MANHATTAN GIRLS

By

J. D. Fitzgerald

authorjdfitzgerald.com

thestoriesofjdandivy.blogspot.com

J. D. Fitzgerald

*Love is nature's way of giving a reason
to be living*

Frank Sinatra, *Love Is A Many Splendored Thing*.

4

Gwen's Diary

ere I am. My eyes staring at the wall and my bags packed by the bedroom door. The past few months have been an emotional roller-coaster, I can't hardly tell which is reality and which is a dream. But now the day has finally arrived for me to leave Statesville for good. I think it would be too soon to break out of here just yet, though I always felt I was destined to leave the state and explore the wonders of the north east. New York City. The Big Apple. The place where all things are possible, and everyone is free to just be themselves. No more Hicksville!
All I can do is look back in this place in memory. Geez, there so much to write about. I don't know where to start. Okay, let's start with the things I'll miss the most: The wide- open spaces. The lush green meadows, flowers blooming in the spring and taking walks at Mac Anderson park, feeling the nature breeze blowing in my hair as the trees rustle softly. But what is dear and close to my heart are my two best friends, Mona and Maxine. We've been through so much together, it feels so wrong to do something this big without them.

Mona was there for me during a stage when I was going through some pretty dark times in my life. The times when my dad would come home in his drunken stupor and fall asleep on the couch, lost in a haze of booze and drugs. My mom, too tired to get into an argument but still worried I'd see him like that, would drape the covers over him and walk away from the situation like sweeping dust under a rug. It would only be a year later until mom filed for divorce.

I know I wrote this many times before, but today I keep thinking of how Mona was the one who got me through all of that. She had some family drama of her own, and by sheer coincidence, that's how we sort of leaned on to each other. We could talk out our problems with each other. We could listen to each other. And from then on, we were fast friends. By the time I met Maxine, my parents were finalizing their divorce, which led to a nasty custody battle. From the sketchy details that I know, my mom had little fight in her and just wanted it all to be over as long as she had full custody of me, but her lawyer really nailed my father. Dad was ordered to take a drug test and when he failed, he was granted only supervised visitation rights and that was only after he completed rehab. But it wasn't like my mom had a choice; this was beyond emotion. She thought about *my welfare* and only my welfare. It's just sad we had to wind up like that.

Things were going well during my early childhood. My dad seemed normal enough, being his nurturing, caring self, though I was too young to see the signs. But as I got older, maybe around nine or ten, his drinking took over. When he drank or did any substance under the sun, he wasn't my kind dad anymore. He was often indifferent to my affection, wholly absorbed by his own sins. The day he lost the custody battle was the beginning of the end. He stayed in rehab for barely a week, said it wasn't his thing. My mom tried to encourage him, she even got certified as a drug counselor and volunteered at a clinic, but it was no use. He packed his bags and made the oh-so-smart decision to move to Georgia with uncle Joe to deal with his addiction on his own. My dad sent me letters for a while, but they were full of promises he couldn't keep, so I pretty much lost faith in him.

Meeting Maxine—being born and bred from an easy, breezy home life in Atlanta---was like a breath of fresh air to me. Her first and only time at a public school was rough on her, so as a solution to her crisis, Mona and I welcomed her with open arms. Through the sixth grade and beyond, we were woven into a circle of three, sharing a sacred bond. But then puberty kicked in, and that's when each and all of us started coming into our own. Nothing really changed with me, or at least I don't think so. It was really Mona and Maxine who were beginning to evolve.

Mona, in an act of rebellion, cut her long brown hair into short spikes, highlighted in red and black and started marking her T-shirts with made-up slogans like "Sex Pistols Rule" or "Hold Me, Thrill Me, Kiss Me, Kill Me." She even got in trouble a few times for wearing such "obscene" shirts; her dad didn't care but our school is notorious for their strict dress code policy. So there goes artistic expression. Maxine wore much more colorful, stylish clothing with the designer labels ever more prominent and adapted a flirter, more outgoing personality. But like I said before, I didn't change at all. I wore the same boring clothes, had the same drab, ashy brown hair, and looked far too young for my age. It's a wonder what puberty can do to you, though, and I consider myself a...late bloomer.

It was the age of high school. And oh boy, freshman year was a tailspin. Gone were the innocent days of childhood, exchanged for the hardships of teenage-hood, as I would like to call it. The personalities of my two close friends became stronger around this period in time. And they'd always, **always** had their differences. Suddenly there was constant bickering and disagreements. And the trouble with me was that I always fall into the middle of their childish fights. Meanwhile, Maxine wanted to be more involved with the rich and popular crowd, stepping further away from the bond we once had. In the long run, it alienated me and frustrated Mona. Things just wasn't the same anymore. The party of three now became a party of two. Us, three musketeers, were still close but not as inseparable as we once were...

So, I'm technically leaving Statesville on a bad note. But it's not like I'll be away from my friends forever, but I just have the feeling of never looking back. This should be my chance to explore a whole new world, to see what's on the outside of the fence. And that's what people do in New York; they look for a purpose in life, something to fulfill their inner desires. Maybe that's what I need to do. Because, life is what you make it, right?

◆ ✳ ✳

NEW YORK, NEW YORK

"Mom, please tell me why we're doing this again?" Gwen Stevenson groaned as she sat back in agitation. The sun gleamed intensely beyond the heavy traffic heading up towards ninety-five east. She rolled down the car window, taking an air of relief as she felt the mid July breeze. It was only a few miles away. The Big Apple. The city that never sleeps. It was all happening so fast, forming fragments in her mind to where time kept up at speed. This was going to be her new home, or what Gwen lead to believe so. But why now? Susan, who had a thirst for adventure, decided to branch out on a mother/daughter road trip by early June, two weeks before school ended, staying from hotel to hotel between West Virginia and Pennsylvania. Gwen had asked her mother countless times about the sudden move. Her only answer was: "Keeping the road up ahead until we reach the key of success." Not the answer she was looking for, though her mom was known to be sanguine philosopher.

It wasn't like her home in Statesville, North Carolina, was anything special. It was an average small town, forever trapped in their false idyllic southern tranquility, when underneath lies a foray of insufferable gossip and hard-hitting financial downfalls. Going to school was sort of a daily routine. Hour by hour, day by day, week by week in a bleak, repetitive disillusionment. Gwen didn't have a terrible time at Statesville High school, but how she would describe it was, tedious. The students would find ways to fulfill their thirst for unnecessary drama by creating outlandish rumors or causing a ruckus on the school football field, which were famous for its make-out spots…and other things. It wasn't about fitting in with certain groups, Gwen hadn't fit in at all, always in the shadow of her more abrasive peers and never standing out or speaking up. Her crippling shyness always defeated her. How would it be any different at the school she was going to in New York? She knew the kids from New York would be much worldlier than her small-town classmates. The city was an unpredictable gateway of unforeseen possibilities waiting to happen that Gwen wasn't sure if she had the same sway of a high-end city girl.

"Like I said, Gwen, we're making a transition," Susan said with calm importance. Her mom had been a writer for the Statesville daily newspaper until that one April afternoon, she made a brass move that made headlines within the state press. Frustrated at the town mayor's empty contribution to the town's high unemployment rate, Susan typed a scandalous article about how businesses were shutting down at the weight of high taxes and regulated zoning laws.

Gwen's mom always had a knack for rallying protesters and fighting injustice but this time it was at the cost of her job. Susan never let it down and continued to fight for her cause, not bowing down to the mayor's bullying tactics. She barely noticed them. But what she also didn't notice was how much damage her activism rained down on Gwen.

Amber Krecther, the mayor's pretty, popular daughter, gave her daily hell. She took advantage of the outlandish rumor brigade, branding Gwen as the topic of any of her conversation and ridiculing her waifish, mousy appearance. A girl like Amber Krecther, with her naturally developed breasts, curtain of luscious blond hair, and statuesque legs, was too perfect to be true, which made her rounds of approval more challenging. If somebody wasn't up to her standards of appearance, she would so easily point out that person's flaws in unapologetic savagery. Every time she went home, she would hide underneath the bedsheets and sob, feeling a sharp clip of her self-esteem breaking into a thousand pieces. But she wasn't the type of kid to blame her mom. She believed in Susan, looked up to her beliefs, and was proud of her. She thought, maybe one day, she would gain her mother's strength. But right now, she was just plain, pathetic Gwen, inside and out, letting her clouded emotions lead the way. Her stringy, long hair was a drab, grayish brown color, her underdeveloped face and figure were completely unremarkable, and her less than stellar wardrobe did her no favors. She thought only Mona and Maxine would ever accept her. Though, of course, it was small town North Carolina. And by North Carolinians' standards, she might one day be considered cute in someone's eyes. But only in an adorable sad-puppy kind of way, not beautiful or even interesting-looking. Adding insult to injury, people often mistook her for being much younger than she was. At age fifteen, Gwen still looked as if she was twelve, which aggravated her to no end.

"You just haven't developed yet," her mother would say. "We Stevensons are late bloomers."

You got that right, Gwen thought. *At least my breasts came in quickly, thank god.*

In the months before the move, Susan received a lot of attention for her protest rallies. One newspaper article named her "Wonder Woman," which had to be one of her former Statesville Daily co-workers congratulating her. Once the evidence came forth of his seedy investment deals with city bank founder Lloyd Stanley, that's when some of the townspeople started turning against Mayor Krecther, who was up for re-election. The incident almost made national news as a crowd of protesting mobs were circling around the Statesville Daily headquarters, decrying Susan's firing. Not long after, Susan began to receive strange emails and envelopes. Some of encouragement and some of hate. Though it was that one beacon of opportunity, permanently printed on a piece of paper, prophesying the ensuing chain of events, but offering only a job.

Then it all boiled down to this: Gwen sitting quietly in their SUV while her mom gripped the steering wheel with determination. Gwen realized there were no questions to be asked. No real straight answer that would satisfy her. So, she sat back and watched the skyscrapers in the distance coming closer and closer, as traffic on the roads steadily increased, Gwen closed her eyes to go back to her reminiscences.

The only thing she'll miss in Statesville, were her best friends, Mona and Maxine. Although the three girls were very different from each other, they always had this unattainable bond and Gwen was the glue that kept them together.

Gwen met Mona in the third grade, fresh off from Raleigh amid her parent's divorce. At first, she was a quiet child, not particularly interested in making friends. It was a tough time for her during that period, and Gwen ironically went through the same thing. All Gwen could remember was her thick long wavy hair that flowed past her shoulders. God, she had such beautiful hair. And she had an inquisitive beauty that any other nine-year-old could not match: Piercing green eyes, a porcelain doll-like face and medium-tanned skin. Gwen was envious. However, there was a deep sadness about her. She never smiled, let alone ever emote to anything. It wasn't like Gwen was the best talker either, but she at least tried to make a friendly greeting with a hello or how are you, but to no avail. When she saw that Gwen was making the effort to interact with her, Mona gave in and greeted back. In some strange serendipity, they became fast friends, mostly because of how much they had in common. They were avid fans of Buffy the Vampire Slayer, had an impassioned love for alternative rock, and would get a kick out of watching mindless slasher movies on Friday nights. Mona was finally comfortable with telling Gwen anything, including times when she witnessed her parents fighting and felt like she had no one else to turn to, going through her grandmother's verbal abuse with no shoulder to cry on and feeling too isolated, too insecure, to be around kids her age because she felt like she wasn't good enough. Once Gwen heard her words, it was like watching a mirror.

One night, while celebrating their monthly slumber parties over Betty and Veronica comics and reruns of *Buffy*, the girls were lounging on the floor of the living room. Mona had a fit of laughs and giggles, Gwen never seen her so happy. But then Mona's laughter died down, her face turning serious yet full of appreciation.

"I'm glad to have you as my friend," Mona said before grasping Gwen in an embrace. They felt like they needed each other more than anything. Whatever problems they had, it would wash over from the adoration of their growing love for each other.

Enter fifth grade. That's when Maxine came along, dressed in her Sunday best, which looked like a French school uniform with a blue beret added to a bow on top. It was her first day of school after all and like many kids arriving in a new town and settling into a new school, Maxine felt very awkward and unsure of herself. She didn't really talk that much, nervously playing with her fingers and barricading herself from everyone. The kids thought she was from another country, let alone another planet. So, over the course of two days, the teasing started, making Maxine feel even worse. Just the sight of her eating at her lunch table in doleful silence caused a sting of empathy from Mona and Gwen.

Maxine was an Atlanta native, who had transferred from a private school, so her father could be near his cookie empire. Although she'd known a lot of kids at her previous school, Maxine really wouldn't consider them as friends. More like friendly acquaintances. At ten years old, Maxine could tell who her real friends were and who weren't. But Mona and Gwen were different.

Sitting at a lunch table, all alone as usual, Maxine was a bit surprised when they joined her. She was quiet most of the time, talking in quick sentences but through the gist of it, the girls were able to make her feel more accepted.

Through the troubling times of entering a public school and dealing with the harsh treatment of the kids, Maxine was shy, soft-spoken, with only a speck of confidence. But somewhere in there, just by the look in her eye, Gwen could see this lively exuberance within her, like a spark of energy waiting to be unleashed.

Maxine felt like she was the belle of the ball when she was around Gwen and Mona. They listened when she talked, they laughed at her jokes, they admired her clothes. They treated her like she was a somebody, and not the poor little rich girl she deemed herself to be. Gwen always reminded her, no matter who she was or what background she came from, they were going to be friends till the end.

Throughout middle school, they suffered together—first braces, first crushes, and most of all puberty. Susan jokingly called them the three musketeers because of how inseparable they were together, and from then on, they accepted the amusing retort by dressing in 16th century costumes one Halloween night. Having special moments like that was a gift to be given. Until high school came that is. Maxine finally got the recognition she craved for as she became more outgoing and amped up her wardrobe. In the meantime, Mona was going through some sort of angry, rebellious phase. They were still friends, of course, but the times they shared were not like they used to be, up until this new path that Gwen wasn't sure she was ready to make.

She snapped her eyes open. Looking back now was so far and distant. The tearful goodbyes, the promises they held so dear to memory's keepsake, telling both no matter what, they would always be the three musketeers, the fearless trio overcoming any obstacles that set their way. But would they have the same bond as they did all those years? Gwen tried to fight back tears. It was so hard not to cry, she grew up with these girls, pouring her whole heart to them, and now she had this agonizing feeling that things weren't going to be the same anymore.

"Change" was a weird word to her. She saw change as a metamorphosis into the grand scale of life and what happened thereafter. Gwen felt shivers down her spine, anticipating this new chapter in her life.

She was here. She could sense it. Once Gwen glanced back at the car window, she could see the shimmering city in the distance, glittering like crystals in the sunlight. It was beautiful. Gwen had always dreamed of coming here, being in a new environment. The capital of the world, no less. Much better than being shacked up in a nowhere town in the south.

Now here she was, jettisoning her way into the city that never sleeps.

And she was ready for it.

◆ ✳ ✳

WELCOME TO HAMILTON ACADEMY

When Gwen thought about their new home, she expected to live in a tiny, roach-infested studio apartment in Hell's kitchen, dreading to deal with constant screaming of the neighbors behind the tattered drywall. Susan had done all right at the *Statesville Daily,* but everybody knew New York was a highly expensive city and whatever paper had hired her mom probably wasn't throwing money at her.

But then they stopped in front of an apartment building on the Upper East Side of Manhattan of all places. Gwen felt out of place in the huge marble lobby as Susan finished her paperwork for their new home. She saw a flock of corporate city executives crossed the sidewalk nearby. The women on the street were sharply dressed in their Saks Fifth Avenue wear while the men were dressed in last season's Calvin Klein's. The mere sight of these people was immaculate.

Gwen was in way over her head in a glitzy place like this. How did she get here? Maybe they had paid her mom extra at the rehab center? She, of course, did work two jobs. Not forgetting how clever her mom can be, she probably saved a quarter of the money for a rainy day. Although she did remember Susan telling her she'd gotten this new job without even applying for it. They just contacted her and offered the position out of the blue. Gwen begin doing some calculations in her head. The salary at the New York Daily times was at least sixty-four thousand, making it a possibility her mom was hired there. Therefore, Susan never pacifically told her where she was hired.

Her mom finished the paperwork and waved Gwen into the elevator where she pushed a button for the twentieth floor. As they stepped out of the elevator and into the new pad, Gwen couldn't believe her eyes.

The place was big and with each spot neatly furnished, shaped up like the perfect IKEA home. The furniture was made into unique patterns, giving off sort of a retro seventies vibe. Her mom was known to be a fan of that decade, so Gwen knew that her style of living would imitate that. The sash living room windows had a great overview of the city, making it the perfect sitting arrangement to gaze at the city lights at night. The sight of it was almost inviting, Gwen couldn't wait to check out her bedroom. It wasn't glamorous or high class, but it was just right. Just right for the two of them. That's when Susan told her the news.

"I got the job at the *New York Times*," she said while the two stood in the foyer of their new home.

"Mom, seriously, you're telling me this *now?*

"I wanted it to be a surprise."

"Okay," Gwen responded simply, shrugging her shoulders carelessly.

"Oh, Gwen, honey, aren't you excited for me?" Susan said in a mock begging tone. "I'm going to have a byline in the *New York Times*. I'm finally being taken seriously as a journalist. You know I put a lot of head and heart into this work. Come on, show your love, doll."

Gwen wrapped her arms around her mom. "Well, honestly, Mom...I couldn't be any prouder. You definitely deserve it."

Susan returned the hug, giving Gwen a huge kiss on the cheek. "Now that's what I wanted to hear."

Later that night, Gwen laid on her bed, wide awake. August fifth was the honorary first day of school. She couldn't help but think of how she was going to present herself. What clothes she would wear? What style she would make her hair? How she would talk without that embarrassing Southern twang in her voice? So many thoughts, so much to prepare for.

Classes were starting in two weeks and she didn't know anything about the school she'd be attending. Would it be an inner-city school with all the violence and whatnot, or worse? Would it be a private school? Gwen shuddered at the thought. A private school full of spoiled, entitled rich kids. Now that was a nightmare on its own.

Gwen's imagination was running wild at this point. All she had to do was close her eyes, turn on her CD player and keep her mind at ease. Two weeks until grind time. It was all but inevitable.

The two weeks had passed by in a rush. When the alarm went off, Gwen sat up in bed, deep in thought. The tension was rising. She didn't want to stay at home any longer. There was no point; she just had to suck it up and hope for the better. There was no reason to step back or be scared, it would be just like any other high school, maybe more fun perhaps. However, socializing with the kids at this school was an immense challenge for her, considering her difficult times adjusting at Statesville high. But this was her chance to start her life over, finally leaving those two embarrassing years behind her.

She investigated the bathroom mirror. Her skin was a little pale, her hair was messy and droopy as ever, her teeth still clamped in the braces she had since she was thirteen. She looked so...unfortunate. She didn't get much sleep from the night before which made her nerves even more erratic. She felt her stomach drop from the moment it came to her mind, that yes, this was the start of her junior year at a New York City school. Though the first thing she had to do was go on proper diet, she was getting far too skinny. The next month after, will be her sixteenth birthday; she must at least look somewhat mature for that age. But then again, puberty wasn't being kind to her. If she looked like a ten-year- old now, there was no becoming of her within the next year. She might reach her peak at twenty-five if she was ever lucky enough. Secondly, she had to get rid of these damn braces. Haven't her teeth straightened out yet? The constant plans of beautifying herself was endless.

Although she tried hard not to think about it, images of her father kept forming in her head. Jack was known to be a handsome man, even her mom didn't deny it, but from how Gwen could describe him, he was a beautiful disaster. When was the last time she spoke to him? Three years? The long distance was putting a deep severance in their relationship. For all Gwen could know, her father was dead to her. There was chance of redemption, a chance to pick up the pieces of his broken promises, but his habit was his burden and she hated him for that. Susan really tried to make the marriage work, being the type of woman to never let a good man down. But as she saw that Gwen was old enough to see the repeated patterns, she knew she had to stop kidding herself. After finishing up divorce court and the custody proceedings, Jack decided to embark on his own selfish journey, claiming to "search for sobriety on his own terms." Gwen seemed to forget that stubbornness ran in her dad's side of the family. He knew he was a disappointment and he was too proud to let his daughter acknowledge that. For now, Jack was living with her good o'l uncle Joe, also a recovering addict, who could fall off the wagon on his bad days and his second wife, Maggie, a saint of a woman who had to put up with a lot of crap that she didn't askfor.

Gwen cleaned her face vigorously with a damp towel. The memories of her father still stung her to the core, good, bad, and all around. Gwen looked into her eyes much more vividly. The color of his hooded sapphire eyes had mixed well with Susan's misty gray's, giving her a distinct aqua color. Her mom would tell her that, when the day she was born, all she could see was the color of the ocean.

"You're going to be a real man-eater one day," Jack would tell her. He sure had a way with words.

Look at me now, Dad, Gwen said in her head. *Am I man-eater yet?* Gwen closed her eyes and turned away in anguish.

She had to focus. The day could go on longer if she wasn't fully prepared. She started rummaging in her wide closet that was big enough to hold all the stuff she'd hauled up from North Carolina. The closet she had back at home had been crammed tight with stuff she'd refused to throw away since childhood. Susan kept telling her to clean it out, but Gwen always managed to put her off. Right now, at this moment, she was lucky to have all her belongings in one place. She pulled out a ratty old trench coat from the Salvation Army that her grandmother gave her. Mama Marge, the head matriarch of the Stevenson family, always had a love of antiques shopping, especially frequent trips to the Salvation Army. And the best thing she could buy for Gwen was this century old trench coat that was excruciatingly heavy on her shoulders. *Talk about the worst birthday present.*

Next stop: dresser.

Gwen begin digging in her antique dresser, picking out any shirts or skirts that would fit her after her most recent growth spurt. She sensed someone behind and quickly turned around. Susan was standing at the door, wearing a red turtleneck sweater with a dark gray blazer paired with pants the same color, her blond hair pulled back in a smart ponytail. She'd never seen her mother so polished.

"Geez, Mom, you scared me," Gwen said, pulling back in surprise.

"Sorry, hon," Susan chuckled.

Gwen sat on the edge of the bed to examine the jumble of clothes. She hated how underage it looked. Since when did she wear Hello Kitty shirts?

"This is an important day," Susan began regally like a news anchor. "Your first day of school. You know, maybe it would be good if you dress nicely for your grand entrance."

"What do you mean nicely?" Gwen asked suspiciously.

"Maybe it would be good if you dressed more prim and proper. I wish you let me take you shopping...Hmm." Susan touched her chin with her finger in thought as she dubiously eyed the pile on the bed. "Why don't you wear that nice sweater your grandmother made you?"

Gwen looked at her mom like she was an idiot. How many times was she was going to have to remind her, she wasn't nine years old anymore. Did her mom really think she should wear that stupid sweater she'd gotten for Christmas five years ago? No way.

"Really, Mom? Are you seriously going to make me wear that?" Gwen said with a look of horror. What made it even more nerve-racking was that she didn't even know what kind of school she was going to yet. So, looking like an overstuffed panda wasn't likely to impress her peers.

"Oh, Gwen, come on. I know it's a little...juvenile, but the color is gorgeous on you and your Grandmother worked hard stitching up that sweater. Please, do her the honor. One day won't hurt, will it? Then we'll go shopping after you've seen what the kids are wearing."

Gwen rolled her eyes and sighed. There was no choice left. The sweater wasn't too bad. Maybe just a thin line from looking plain and unattractive, a little itchy, well a lot itchy, but she'd pull through. Though the most important thing was, she wanted to go to school. She kind of liked school. And she was ready for something to do. Keep her occupied, more focused. Susan would hassle her until she wore the damn sweater, so why fight it? There
was no other option than to wear it, in accordance with her mother's wishes. Or Grandma Marge's wishes.

Gwen sighed dramatically. "Okay."

Susan gave Gwen a big bear hug. "Grandma will be so excited, I just have to send her a picture. Now let's hurry up and get ready. I gotta be at work in twenty minutes."

"Mom, exactly what kind of school am I going to?" Gwen curiously asked.

Susan slyly pressed her fingers to her lips. "Shh. It's a surprise."

Gwen had a feeling this wasn't going to be a good surprise.

During a rather quick taxi ride, with no sign of heavy traffic in the way, they reached the school entrance at 1365 York Ave, right close to the Optimum rehab center. Gwen tried to make out the words grandly emblazoned on the top of the building.

HAMILTON ACADEMY

She wasn't sure if she was familiar with this particular school. She had learned of someone named Roy Hamilton in history class, a famed scholar who founded a school in New York after his journey from Europe in 1775.

Wow. If it was the same guy, Gwen was going to a school that changed history. Oh, how lucky she was becoming. But still, she didn't know what kind of school she was enrolling in. She felt her palms sweating. The suspense was killing her.

She saw a group of young women walking along the building dressed in the latest fashions. If Gwen would ever think of the designer names…Gucci, Prada, Versace, Kelli Martin…Then it hit her. These were not professional young twenty-somethings. These were teenage girls! Going to *her* school. Her heart sank. Normally, she wouldn't be caught dead in the outfit she was wearing now: the ratty trench coat, the dopey sweater (courtesy of Grandma Marge) and a not-so-sexy plaid skirt with black tights and scuffed sneakers. Her defined freak status was full stamped and ready. There was no way she was stepping inside that building. At least not dressed like this.

"Uh, Mom, do you know what kind of dress code this school has?" Gwen asked worriedly, even though she already knew.

"It's a private school, sweetheart. Although, you don't have to wear those ridiculous uniforms some of these schools require, it's highly prestigious and upstanding and students are expected to dress the part. Don't worry, hon. With your good grades, you'll fit right in."

Gwen stared at the statue of a bespectacled, bearded man holding a scroll. Yep, it was the scholar known as Roy Hamilton. And this was definitely a private school. Gwen shut her eyes to summon up whatever courage she had. Her legs were shaking uncontrollably as she got out of the taxi, and from then on, she bid her mom goodbye. *Okay, let's make the best of it.*

The kids were hanging out full front and center of the school. They stared at her in bewilderment, repulsed by her strange appearance.

Gwen counted to ten. The day would start, go from beginning to end, and it'd all be over. It was going to be eight hours in hell.

◆ * *

MEETING YOUR PEERS

After third period, it was finally lunchtime. Gwen could definitely use a breather. She pulled out her class schedule while standing in the cafeteria, looking for a place to sit.

First Period—Geography

Second Period—English

Third Period—Calculus

Fourth Period—Science

One of her favorite subjects since middle school was English; it almost made the morning bearable. The topic of discussion was Shakespeare, though the focus was geared towards his much lighthearted *A Midsummer Night's Dream,* a change of pace from the usual gloomy *Hamlet* or *Romeo and Juliet.* Right around the time when Gwen was eleven, she wasn't an avid fan of his at first, trying to comprehend the nonsensical dialogue and endless plot threads that reeked of cliché. But one day as she and her mom made a trip to Barnes And Nobles, she discovered a book that featured Shakespeare's literary work in art form. And, she just got *hooked.* She couldn't put the book down. The paintings beautifully illustrated the complexity of his storytelling, blending in well into the fantastical visuals he displayed in his writing. Gwen had an immediate respect for the playwright ever since. She must've kept that book somewhere. Maybe it was in her closet? Reality sunk in and Gwen caught herself standing at the lunch line like a dazed idiot, habitually getting lost into her thoughts again. She noticed the kids constant staring and snickering as they gave away occasional glances. Feeling her anxiety cave in on her, Gwen darted across the cafeteria, desperately trying to find a table to sit at.

On the far right, she saw a girl sitting alone, reading an encyclopedia or something equally huge. She recognized her as Kyle Durmsdale from her Calculus class. She had a peculiar look about her. A cute angular face with lips perched in stern concentration and as she looked up at every page, Gwen could see the color of her eyes shifting from emerald to forest green. She was one of those academic overachievers, strict and direct in her approach. Her clothing style was modest, dressed in a blue striped button-down under a cardigan gray sweater with a wool gray skirt to match. Her dark auburn hair was braided into a tightly-knit ponytail, her eyes emotionless through her oval-shaped lens.

Every question Mr. Alverson had asked, she raised her hand in a quick robotic fashion. she answered each question correctly, three times in a row. Gwen had been impressed. This Durmsdale girl was quite the sharp shooter. And from the look of her envious classmates, she was not above stepping a few toes to get her way. How come she wasn't sitting with the honor society kids? Or at least Gwen thought those were the honor society kids, she wasn't sure. Maybe the girl just liked sitting by herself—or maybe she wouldn't mind some company. Gwen decided to join her. The girl did seem quiet and harmless enough, although Gwen had to be careful not get on the girl's bad side. She kind of came off as intimidating.

"Mind If I sit here?"

There was complete silence. She didn't acknowledge Gwen in any way. She was so busy reading that damn book. A chemistry book, no less.

NOT really a good conversation starter, Gwen thought as she sat and picked her food. She had a hotdog, chips, baked beans, and yogurt. Earlier, a girl in the lunch line had glared at Gwen's plate in disgust, as if she was carrying a whole shitload of unhealthy junk food. Gwen had a healthy appetite, like most *normal* people do, and had a relatively slim, although quite skinny, waist. What was so wrong with having a good lunch occasionally? She hadn't even had breakfast, for Christ sakes.

Gwen stared blankly at the walls of the cafeteria. She was bored out of her mind. Back at her old school, the only exciting thing was—no, not food fights—Channel 1, some news program for teens, appearing on the television the school installed near the ceiling. Now, five-hundred miles apart from North Carolina, she was sitting here with a girl who barely emoted or spoke while everyone else avoided her like the plague. This was going to be her life now. Only if she'd let it be.

Just as Gwen finished the rest of her hot dog, someone caught her eye. A boy with dark brown hair sat at a table up front, not so far from Gwen's view. He was dressed in the usual preppy attire, wearing a green sweater vest over a white button-down and khaki slacks. From the look of his chiseled features, he looked older than he was. Gwen can only guess he was a senior boy, heading close to at least sixteen to seventeen years of age. When she caught a glance of his eyes, she almost melted. The color was a deep midnight blue, which gleamed brightly under the florescent lights of the cafeteria. When the boy shifted his eyes toward Gwen, she looked down at her tray. Nervous knots were shooting through her stomach. She glanced up again, and this time, the boy was staring right at her.

He probably thinks I'm a freak, Gwen thought gravely. She felt like a disjointed statue, an artist's mistake, this skinny, bony, frail little thing that would never come close to attracting a boy. Who knew what was going on in this boy's mind? What did he really think of her? She ran her fingers through her hair, not in a flirtatious way, just one of her little nervous ticks she would get to stop her body from shaking. Who was she kidding? She was a complete joke. Plain and simple.

Surprisingly, he made a slight grin.

Gwen couldn't help to smile back but had to be careful not to show her braces. He was so dreamy, but Gwen couldn't help to wonder why he was so interested in her, on the account of how she wasn't as well-groomed as the other girls.

Then the doors burst into the cafeteria and the silent flirting stopped dead. Now the boy was pretending to have a conversation with a guy who was seated next to him, wearing the same identical Abercrombie and Fitch wear, except with jet-black hair smoothed to the side.

All Gwen could hear was excited loud whispers as the kids turned their heads towards the entrance. She turned around to see what the hubbub was about. A girl with a shower of raven black hair joined the second table from above. She looked rather mature, wearing her Ralph Lauren blouse and a tight brown knee-length pencil skirt. Two other girls came in, an African-American wearing a Diane Von Furstenberg wrap dress and a strawberry blond who looked too skinny in her Betsy Johnson outfit. The raven-haired girl eased beside the boy with the midnight blues, running her fingers through his hair. Great, he had a girlfriend. She knew guys like that wouldn't be up in the market for too long.

Gwen looked around the cafeteria and then gazed at the clock. Fifteen minutes left. Gosh, how could her first day be so bleak when it was only halfway over? She turned her attention to the girl who was reading her chemistry book. *When is she ever going to put that book down? Does she even talk at all?* Gwen had no choice.

Although she knew it was rude, she knocked on the table to get the girl's attention. The girl lifted her head slightly and gave Gwen a hard stare, as if she'd be damned if anyone interrupted her studying. Gwen had both of her hand firmly on her legs, biting her bottom lip. Okay, it was done, she definitely got on this girl's bad side.

The girl flipped the book closed. "Now I lost my train of thought," she said brusquely.

"I'm...I'm sorry. I just wanted to say hi," Gwen stuttered nervously.

The girl scanned around the cafeteria room in disdain. Then she looked back at Gwen and squinted her brow, trying to remember something. "Hey, aren't you in my calculus class?" It almost sounded like an accusation.

"Um, Yeah."

"Sorry if I wasn't being friendly, I tend to be kind of intense," the girl said in a softer, more approachable tone. "I really don't trust most of the kids in the school, though human instinct is what you go by. Are you new here?"

"Yeah, I moved here from North Carolina." Gwen smiled. She was actually sparking up a conversation with someone. Maybe making friends here wouldn't be a difficult task after all.

"So, what's your name?"

"Gwen Stevenson."

"Interesting," the girl said. "My name is Kyle Durmsdale. I know I have a weird last name. Most often, people call me Drumsdale to make it sound even more embarrassing; Though it's mostly intentional. Sorry if I'm rambling, I don't want to bore you to death." The girl let out a girlish chuckle, her stone-cold façade beginning to melt in a warm, accepting glow. Suddenly, Gwen's nervous shivers begin to wind down.

"Oh, it's cool. How come you're sitting here alone and not with the honor society group?" Gwen asked curiously. "You seem pretty bright."

Kylie sighed gravely. "Well, I'm too smart for my own good."

"That's bogus," Gwen chuckled incredulously. "Who would say that?"

"Just ask Bianca Walworth," Kyle seethed.

"Who?"

Kyle pointed to the raven-haired girl in front of them. "She's the president of the honor society. When she found out my GPA was slightly higher than hers, she thought of ways to block me out of joining at all. Jealously is a highly common thing at this school."

Gwen glanced at the table again. The boy with the midnight blues caught her stare. She held his gaze, entranced. But soon the raven-haired girl caught her infatuated glance and her violet cat-eyes flashed. It was like a laser shooting at her. She suddenly knew why the boy with the midnight blues would fall in love with this girl. She had the most impressive pair of eyes Gwen had ever seen, a royal purple color with a speck of green to give a turquoise hue. Gwen hadn't known anybody with a pair of eyes like that since, well, heck, Elizabeth Taylor. She also had the beauty and grace of Ava Gardner, complete with a pearl necklace and an amethyst ring around her index finger.

Gwen, in all her life, have never seen a girl so polished and pristine; she looked as though she was from another time. She gazed at the girl with both adoration and trepidation.

The girl's eyes narrowed, giving her the meanest glare. She held the boy with the midnight blues firmly around his arm, as if protecting him from Gwen.

"Don't make eye contact," Kyle warned, interrupting her thoughts. "You'll get on her bad side."

"I think I already have," Gwen said dolefully. *Way to go, Gwen.*

There were so many Amber Krecthers that every kid had to deal with. But this girl, had just the right malice and vindictiveness to make every one of them count. If looks could kill, she would be a mass murderer.

Gwen could only prepare for the worst.

ENTER BIANCA WALWORTH

Bianca Walworth sat confidently at her lunch table, knowing she looked good. Hair primed, makeup spotless, and the perfect attire for the day. She still couldn't stop glancing at the feeble-looking girl at the "nerd" table. Cause who else would sit there but Kyle Durmsdale, having her "nerd" status carved in stone. Though, this one peculiar girl had her attention for some reason. She resisted to look away from the creepy big eyes masking behind a perturbed, juvenile face hiding behind strands of plain ash-tray brown hair. To top it all off, she had the tackiest fashion. A dumpy blue sweater, a plaid checkered green skirt that had escaped from the seventies and those awful black tights. She was so weird-looking, to the point where it put an enormous strain on Bianca's eyes.

What made it even stranger was the freak kept staring at Chace. *Her Chace.* For Bianca, it was hard to accept the fact that he was the apple of every girls' eye.

Chace Fairbanks came from a family legacy to solidify his golden boy status. His last name alone was the stuff of historical treasury. His great- grandfather was Douglas Fairbanks Jr. who served as a naval officer in world war two and was a successful movie producer in Hollywood but mostly known for having a brief marriage to Joan Crawford. He was almost the spitting image of him in his younger days. Every girl wanted him for herself, however, Bianca was the lucky one. She knew him better than any other girl could. As fate would have it, their fathers were former college buddies, keeping up connections with each other ever since. She even remembered first meeting him at three years old, showing off his overabundant rambunctious energy whenever they horse played in Bianca's toy room. She warmed at the thought of that memory. It'd been so long ago since she had the toy room, which sadly been marginalized into an isolated study filled with books her parents don't even read.

"You're getting quite too old for the toy room, dear," said the phlegmatic voice of her mother. She was just shy from eleven years old when they decided on that. Life goes on after all.

Though right they were when she started looking at Chace in a different way. it was around the age of thirteen when she saw him, slowly but surely, growing into his manhood. He was very active during the summer, so by fall he started to gain more stamina, especially after he took interest in swimming. His midnight blues were beginning to stand out, his face more chiseled, and his voice deepened. As Bianca was having her own bouts with puberty, it was hard to keep Chace off her mind. Her friend, her special little playmate, was now all grown up. She'd known him for over ten years and still she felt all giddy and awkward, even blushed whenever he walked by. Though, it wasn't long before he realized his feelings for her, too. By the start of eighth grade, she ran into him at a mixer. He was a strapping tall freshman then, reaching the peak of his athletic stature. As he asked her to dance, Bianca could just remember how it was like to fall in love for the first time. After the dance, the two of them took a brief walk at Central Park with the view of the city so bright, it glittered like diamonds. It was so majestic. So...romantic. Once their lips met in that first kiss, magic happened. Bianca and Chace became Hamilton academy's golden couple ever since.

She'd seen Chace's body plenty of times in the Hamptons, when they took a swim in the family pool or relaxed under the sun, watching his abs glistening. Being the swim captain did wonders for his build, though, she hadn't yet given herself to him. To Bianca, her virginity was sacred. If she ever did the deed, it would have to be special: special place, special time, everything special. Now, the wait was over. She wanted to envelop passionately into Chace's embrace while the moon painted brightly on a clear starry night, exploring every part of his body. Bianca was more than ready to take the next step.

She now focused her attention on the strange girl, being accompanied by the social pariah Kyle Durmsdale. Kyle was one of those girls who would wear the frumpiest clothes, yet she carried herself like she was the smartest person alive. It was annoying. Those kinds of girls would never wear makeup, or proper shoes, and would never let their hair down, metaphorically speaking. Calling them nerds wouldn't faze them in the least, wearing it like some sort of complimentary badge. Every time Bianca went to her honor society meetings, half the girls were Kyle Durmsdale clones. Those girls, so headstrong and so competent, relishing in their pride with their smarts and not with their looks. They often questioned Bianca's position as honor society president and scoffed at girls who were confident in showing their natural beauty, as if they were brainless bimbos— but why couldn't she be pretty *and* smart? It was an act of arrogance Bianca couldn't understand herself. Through the pure luck of rules and regulations, Bianca was surely satisfied when she told Mrs. Tingleton, the honor society advisor, that Kyle wasn't qualified to join the honor society because of her lack of extracurricular activities. Kyle was a social outcast, that's what she wanted and that's what she got. But choosing not to fit in, did have its consequences. And Bianca wasn't shy about enforcing them. So, Kyle was unable to join the honor society. Too bad. Bianca was the top winner of the game, heck, she was the freakin' president. She wasn't going to let Kyle's high IQ get in the way.

But it looks like Kyle Durmsdale had recruited a new accomplice. How fetching. Perhaps she was that kind of girl, but maybe she was new here and Kyle's table was the only one she could find, the poor thing. Maybe she was a freshman? No, she carried herself a bit too maturely, though she looked awfully young. Far as Bianca could tell, she was fresh breed being picked apart by Sondra Parkas and her cronies Isabella Compton and Blake Kingston.

"God, look at what she's wearing," Sondra gawked. "Her mom must've dressed her."

"She looks like a mental patient," Isabella chimed in, giggling.

"How high is that skirt, by the way?" Blake said, sneaking a glance under the table the girl was sitting.

Isabella playfully punched Blake in the arm. "Oh, Blake, you're such a perv."

Bianca took a moment to examine the girl once more. "She looks kind of sad. Pathetic in a way." She made a light chuckle. "This school is going to eat her alive."

Bianca gazed over at Chace, quizzically.

Chace went on eating his lunch and gave Bianca a vaguely odd look. "What?"

"Any comments," Bianca prompted.

"I don't gossip, babe. That's what girls do."

"Hey, I'm not a girl," Blake whined in a mock-offended tone.

Sondra and Isabella giggled profoundly.

Bianca could've sworn that Chace was ogling at the girl. Why her? This unimpressive little thing, with her greasy hair and god-awful sense of style, who was probably one of those scholarship rejects. Why would she compare herself to her?

The bell suddenly rang. Bianca wanted to give one simple message to Chace before she went off. She held his hand and looked into his dreamy eyes. She'd been planning to tell him this for the longest time.

"I want to do something special," she whispered hopefully. "Maybe next Friday...At the Plaza hotel?"

Chace lifted an eyebrow suggestively. "What's the occasion?"

"It's a surprise, silly," Bianca giggled girlishly.

Chace wrapped his free arm around her waist, giving her a long passionate kiss. "I knew you'd be ready," he whispered back in her ear. Then he strolled out of the cafeteria, leaving Bianca breathless.

To keep herself from fainting, she shook her head and walked along to mesh in with the crowd of people exiting. Someone suddenly bumped into her. Bianca jumped back and found herself staring down at the feeble girl, her googly doll-like eyes creepily pierced into her.

"Can you watch where you're going next time?" Bianca scolded

"Sorry," the girl murmured weakly, rushing away.

She stood so small next to her. So fragile. Bianca was naturally tall and wearing pointed-heeled Manolo Blahniks, no less. She felt so superior. So empowered, that she could make any girl squirm, intently. Furthermore, this girl was new here and everyone else knew the real deal.

Bianca Walworth was the queen of Hamilton Academy. And she sort of liked that title.

THE CONEY ISLAND HIDEOUT

Gwen escaped from the compounds of her boring anatomy assignment and into the school library. She always reverenced the library as a place of sanctuary, to read into the words of a good novel, in ease of her wearied mind.

The smell of fine pinewood soothed Gwen's senses. It was that mutual feeling of comfort, that kind of feeling where you want to sit by a fireplace and drink a cup of coffee, all in the safety of your own...home. Gwen had to admit, she was a little homesick. The city was nothing like a taking a walk through the forest woods, embellishing in its serene scenery as the Rocky Mountains was near far. Though the interior of the school library was much like the one back in Statesville, it was constructed on a larger scale. The room was filled with rows and rows of books to no end, it even had upstairs for the non-fiction area. The design of the lobby was painted in old-fashioned elegance, to which, without any regards, as to why Hamilton gained its educational reputation.

Prestigious with a capital P.

By the dawn of fourth period, Gwen, unfortunately, had to walk up three flights of stairs to get to science class. Walking up those many stairs was straining enough, so Gwen made a run for it, which resulted in her stumbling down while hearing sounds of hysterical laughter. This was the worst possible first day. It was all too scary for her, adapting into a different lifestyle too far from the proximity of her small-town roots.

Gwen plowed her way to the never-ending rows of bookcases. It was like being in a maze, getting lost in every direction. But she didn't mind, all she wanted to do was search for a book to re-evaluate her solitude.

*The Catcher in the Rye by*J. D. Salinger. An all-time classic about a young man alienated by the superficial world of New York City. If only Holden Caulfield was a real person.

As Gwen begin to read Holden's cynical narration of his existence in the privileged world, it resonated with her in such a poetic way. If there was a Holden Caulfield, she would marry him in an instant.

Across from the second row of the reading table, a rather gloomy-looking boy was writing vigorously in his notebook. He had a skinny frame, but Gwen could see the muscles pumping in his biceps. His hair was lush, full of curly reddish-brown cut right above his eyebrows. Once he looked up, his eyes met Gwen's. They were a soft brown color, like chocolate chips melt in honey. They were so soulful. So warm. Gwen couldn't help but smile—not showing her teeth though. Whenever there was a boy involved, in any situation, it was always best to conceal those hideous braces she had. The moment he noticed her, Gwen tried hard to impress him with her sophisticated preen. The ginger-haired boy smiled back, a red glow forming in his cheeks. Beguiled by his sweet boyish smile, Gwen hid behind her book, holding back fits of girlish giggles. Maybe her illusions were in the air, for never-the-less, Gwen never really saw herself as a knockout. Two boys looked at *her*. Yes, two. They examined her in a way of curious fascination, though who knows, through Gwen's diffident mind, they were more so amused by her unfettered appearance. This was indeed a preparatorial facility, competency in looks and attire was an important factor. But as she looked up from her book, there was an innocence to him that she didn't really see in most teenage boys. But behind that soft demeanor lie a mysterious aura, an intensity that was dying to break out at any second. It made him so...enticing.

"I see you're reading *Catcher in The Rye.*"

Gwen jumped back from her reverie and saw Kyle Durmsdale standing beside her. She was holding a tote of books in her hand and sat down, smiling graciously at Gwen. "I didn't know you were that kind of girl."

Gwen squinted at her inquisitively. "What kind of girl would I be?"

"Oh, let's just say 'a slave to classic literature.' Most of the kids at this school think it's pretentious schlock."

"Well when you really look deep into it, it's actually a portrait of the disaffected youth in the eyes of one character, whether he's likable or not. It's also a deconstruction of nineteen-fifties teens and how the world views them. So, I think it's very influential of its time." Gwen sort of surprised herself, she couldn't believe she said all those words in one sentence.

Kyle arched an eyebrow, clasped her hands together like a proud schoolteacher. "Well I guess somebody did their homework."

"That only came out naturally. It's really one of those books that make you think. I read it back in my freshman year and I've loved it ever since."

"I remember *Jane Eyre* being my main obsession back in the seventh grade. Well-written pieces like that have a hold on you," Kyle said. "I didn't know books were an interest of yours."

Gwen chuckled. "Well, it's better than TV, I'll give you that."

"And to think my parents don't even own TV," Kyle chuckled. "But, I've got other things to pass my time, like studying." She stood up firmly. "You want to go to the Hillside Café? I'm meeting a tutor there."

Gwen was flabbergasted. Someone actually wanted to hang out with *her*? "Um, sure."

Kylie checked her watch. "The subway takes about an hour, so we'll have to hurry."

"An hour?!" Gwen said, petrified, not particularly having the experience of being on a subway ride, let alone going to a whole different area of the city.

"Don't worry, I know my way around."

Before Gwen scurried after Kyle, she looked at the brown-eyed boy once more. Their eyes locked. She felt the flutter in her heart. He waved gently as Gwen forlornly waved back.

Gwen's conscience was ascending into a blissful daydream, hoping that one day, fate would lead her back to him.

The subway ride was something of unusual experience. From the homeless performer singing for change to the oddball dressed in the strangest getup out of a weird off-Broadway show, it was one of those unforeseeable moments that had to be written in a diary. Gwen kept reminding to herself that she wasn't in the safe woods of North Carolina anymore. She was in a much bigger, broader city that was beyond her horizon. She had to get over her anxiety somehow, even though the atmosphere was unnerving. Kyle was quiet as usual, scanning words into her history book. She finally put her book back in her tote and turned to face Gwen, her razor-sharp eyes in undeviating attention.

"Okay, just to be a word of mouth, that boy you were staring at in the cafeteria, his name is Chace Fairbanks," she said in low whisper. "His last name is pretty famous around school."

Gwen was sort of caught off guard by Kyle's need to insert the conversation with gossip. "Should I care?"

"Not that you should, but from my research, his long list of family members does have a prominent stance in the Hollywood and Wall street industry, oh how it fascinates me. Though nothing goes asway like goods looks and charm to keep him up float, but, don't get your hopes high.. He's off limits."

Gwen laid her head back in remembrance, picturing the beautiful raven-haired girl and how she kept clinging to the boy's arm. "Never even had him on my mind, but yes, I definitely know."

"I just don't want you to think you're in this clichéd high school fantasy where he would end up with you instead. Practically all the girls dream about being in Bianca's shoes," Kyle said matter-of-factly. "Hey, who knows? Bianca and Chace might have this terrible breakup, which would give him the freedom to find his rebound victim. But I'm not giving you any ideas. Pretty boys like Chace Fairbanks are bad news. And guys like that always go for the delicate, demure types, because, you know, they're more willing. I'm only telling you this for your own good."

"Thanks, I guess," Gwen said, a bit flattered by Kyle's sincerity. "Why the sudden concern though?"

"You're not as self-indulgent or arrogant as I expected you to be," Kyle said simply. "If that was the case, I would've let you embarrass yourself. But you have a certain dignity about you. Or let me put it this way, humble. Easy-going. That's something I respect."

Gwen smiled generously. She only met Kyle twice and already there was beginning to be a spark of trust.

"What part of North Carolina are you from, exactly?" Kyle asked.

Gwen hesitated. "Statesville."

"Hmm. interesting...FYI, though, being in the Big Apple and all, it's all about fitting in. Whether you choose to or not, it's up to you."

Gwen nodded. What she had seen in the past two weeks was the concept of the New York lifestyle. But how could she fit into such a cosmopolitan environment?

"How do *you* fit in, if you don't mind my asking?"

"I don't need to," Kyle prompted proudly. "I have the brains and stride to get me to Harvard one day. Why should I care about some popularity contest? But you, being raised in the country, it's going to take you a while to learn the ropes. Excel or degrade yourself? That is the question."

Gwen leaned against the window, hopelessly. She didn't know how she would cope in a city like New York. It was all so intimidating, the allure of it all. She was glad to have met someone like Kyle. She was headstrong in her own quiet, determined way. Gwen could see the beauty in her, but Kyle refused to let other people see that. There was pride in her self-worth, wanting to be known for her intellectual attributes instead of physical attributes. She came off as a little TOO serious, but Gwen easily passed it off as a personality trait. Most girls back in her hometown would worry about how they looked or how they acted or how they spoke. Insecurity seemed to be a major factor in a teenager's life, but Kyle wasn't prone to that. It took a lot of intelligence and bravery to gain such resilience. It was something she saw in her two best friends, Mona and Maxine, accumulating their abrasive spontaneity. That's the kind of person Gwen wanted to be, though not all the courage in the world could break her out of her cold, dark mental shell.

The train stopped at its destination, with a crowd load of people waiting at the subway district. It was chaotic! Gwen almost lost her balance, trying to keep up the pace of the ongoing passengers rudely shoving and pushing, scrambling out of the cab. Thinking she'd lost Kyle in the ambush, Gwen found her sitting calmly on a bench.

"I don't see how you go on a one-hour train ride every day," Gwen said between breaths.

"Boy, you really are new here, huh?" Kylie quipped nonchalantly.

"I thought I was gonna die out there."

"Just keep calm and wait to make room when you really need to. My tutor suggested we take our studies in this side of town. Thankfully, I only come here on occasion."

"So, who is this person?"

"You'll know her when you see her."

Escaping from the claustrophobic cave of the subway district, Gwen relished in the cool, crisp summer air, admiring the view of Coney Island. It reminded her of the days where her dad used to take her out to Wilmington beach, knowing once, there were always good memories of him. It gave Gwen such a sense of tranquility, looking out at the warm colors of red and orange forming in the distant ray of sunlight as she would hear waves crashing into the sandy grounds.

Gwen followed Kyle towards Neptune ave, reaching to their destination in a discreet alleyway. It was a pub nearby a closed down clothing store, with loud music and boisterous laughter from a mile away. Gwen halted. The panic through Gwen's blood cells ran cold, wrapping her trench coat tighter. There was just something dangerous about this side of town. Why would Kyle, of all people, bring her to a place like this? It was a questionably delirious sight. Seeing what seems to be a well-to-do girl, bragging about her efforts of achieving a law degree, walk casually into what appears to be a bar, five leaps apart from legal age. Gwen had to make an excuse somehow, the thought of going inside that place gave her an alarmed feeling. Maybe it was a good time to call her mom in case anything bad happens. By the time Susan picked up the phone, Gwen could hear the shouting in the background, different voices debating back and forth. The exhaustion in Susan's voice, detailed how working at a New York Newspaper column was a gruesome task.

"Wow, so you're making friends already," Susan said breathlessly.

"Yeah it looks like it." Gwen chuckled. "How come you're so out of breath?"

"It's been quite a hectic day. A story must be written in a span of twenty minutes if I'm lucky. I'm starting small but hopefully I'll get the big articles soon. Wish me luck."

"Just keep up the good work, mom, it'll come soon." Gwen checked her watch. "I gotta go. Love ya."

"Love you, too, sweetie. Promise you'll get home soon."

"I promise."

Gwen stared at the building from across the street. Why wait for the outcome, when she could just get it over with in a span of time? She bravely fastened her trenchcoat, closing her eyes as she marched at the door.

Inside, the place was packed with an outpouring of young adults settled into each section. There was a pool table, a jukebox and a serving table from the corner side. The atmosphere was more akin to a seedy dance club, not exactly a place where one can study. Gwen insinuated that there was probably some underage drinking going on once she spotted one of the kids sneaking in beer and flasks of whisky from under their jackets. A cloud of smoke erupted on the other side where a group of two boys and two girls were necking each other. Another girl swayed her hips rather suggestively to a Maroon 5 song while the boys stared in awe of her. Lastly, a group of college frat boys laughed drunkenly at each other's fart jokes while playing beer pong. The kids seemed more normal than Gwen expected. A bit on the trashy side, but normal none-the-less. Detecting their loud heavy accents, they were mostly kids from New Jersey and Long Island, however, their aura was less intimidating than the kids at Hamilton.

As she walked outside, she come to find Kyle sitting with a girl, looking bored and dazed while gluing her eyes on a clip of notes, ignoring Kyle's reprimands to pay attention. Her dark olive skin registered an air of middle eastern descent. Her short brown hair was gelled up in porcupine spikes, her eyes laced in black eyeshadow, her lips painted black. Wearing a black camisole under a black leather jacket with army pants and boots, from the looks of it, she looked like she escaped from a boot camp. Kyle tapped on the table, pestering her again to pay attention. The girl glared in response instead, pulling out a cigarette.

"Oh, there you are," Kyle said in a huff. "What took you so long?"

"Well, I didn't think you would study at a place like this?" Gwen replied incredulously.

"Okay, sure, I wouldn't particularly study here for my mid-season exam, but I'll do anything to get *her* ass in gear." Kyle pointed to the spiky-haired girl, sitting next to her as the girl rolled her eyes in annoyance. "Oh, where are my manners, Gwen I would like you to meet Vera, my tutor for the day. And Vera, I would like you to meet Gwen, she's new at Hamilton."

The girl pulled out her hand in goofy defiance. "Vera Hudgens. Not related to Vanessa," she greeted, her voice husky with a slight accent.

Kyle made a disapproving smirk at her lit cigarette. "I thought you were going stop smoking those cancer sticks. And I think we ought to choose the library to keep with our studies. You know Ms. Chapman is really gunning you to get a passing grade in chemistry and being here is only going to distract you more."

"Okay, *Mom*," the other girl mocked. "First of all, I haven't smoked in two weeks. Second of all, these are *Gitanes,* a special brand of French cigarettes; I think I'm a little classier than that, Ky. And third, the view is beautiful, the air feels nice, of course this is the perfect spot to study. And my school assignments are all under control. I'm sure Ms. Chapman would understand."

"Fine." Kyle sighed, rolling her eyes. "It's best if we keep our studies *outside* then." She pulled out her books, preparing for the session. "I suggest you take some notes just in case."

"So, Gwen," Vera began, as she waved off Kylie. "Are you from here?"

"I'm originally from North Carolina, me and mom just traveled here a few weeks ago."

"Oh cool, you're a mountain girl," Vera gushed in keen interest. "Ever tried rock climbing?"

Gwen smiled shyly. "Never thought about it."

Vera took drag off her cigarette. "Yeah, I like that nature shit. Really opens the mind, you know."

Those words never spoke truer. Gwen liked how straight-forward this girl was and out of curiosity, she sneaked a peek at the file of papers she was reading.

At Love's Lost by Vera Hudgens.

It was movie script! Wow, this was an artist. A dreamer, a thinker, a believer. Gwen so longingly wanted to join in a crowd like that, a society where she can express her mind and chase her goals. She always wanted to write, expressing her feelings through her little notebook trinket she had since the age of twelve. Her passion was there, but the moment wasn't happening yet. Her true calling was near, but no energy to keep up the flow in life. However, she felt her life's journey taking a path, by experiencing this new adventure that was set up for her. Like her grandmother used to say, "the sun shines brightest on a cloudless day."

"What brings you to Hamilton? Scholarship?" Vera asked.

Gwen expected to hear that question. It was all in a rush how the first day went and wearing an outfit straight from the salvation army raised a lot of heads. It wasn't too prim but it wasn't too *proper* either. But her question was not of any malice. "No, it was sort of last ditch effort from my mom once we came here."

"Surprises are a lot to handle," Vera retorted. "But it was my choice to apply to Hamilton. Last minute decision on my part."

At first glance, she didn't seem like a student at Hamilton. She was too radical and edgy for the Upper East Side crowd. If anything she would fight against the powers that be. However, Gwen, being a country girl at heart, knew that the rules and regulations about fitting in was such a daunting obstacle to take. She begin to discard any attempts of getting involved with such an opulent lifestyle.

"Oh gosh, Ky. I'm sorry I didn't make it to lunch. I was working on these fliers," Vera said to Kyle once it came to her.

"What kind of fliers?"

Vera pulled out a pile of purple-colored sheets of paper. It was printed in big, bold letters that read, ACTRESS WANTED FOR SHORT FILM. A very distinct design of the Oscar statue was below, the two dramatic faces pasted on each side. "For the first time, I plan to film something more than just ten minutes. I mean this has to be epic for me."

Kyle was beginning to be slightly annoyed but went along with it. "So, what is this particular film about?"

"It's a marvelous love story about a fair maiden and a wounded knight," Vera boasted dramatically. "Only the maiden's true love for the knight could save him from his last breath of life. It is titled...At Love's Lost. It's very artistic...Very avant-garde.

Kyle's reaction was that of a blank stare, not entirely fazed. "That's all fine and dandy, Vera, but we really need to get on with our studies. The chemistry quiz is only a week away."

"You're not taking me seriously," Vera said, disappointed.

In concern for Vera's feelings, Kyle softened. "Vera, I support you, I really do but this is why you're getting so distracted. Take time to balance your schedule. Goals and ethics go hand in hand."

Vera rolled her eyes, shoving her fliers into her backpack. "Ky, you're a pain in the ass."

"Just looking out for you."

The bells on Gwen's cellphone begin to ring. Through quick premonition, she sensed that it was her mother, and by looking at the screen, her senses were right. Seven minutes and sixteen seconds. Although it was a normal thing Susan wisely did, Gwen felt like she was being a bit of a worry-wart. As it may be, being the only daughter she has, Susan would always have this fierce protective clutch, almost to the point of seclusion. "Sorry, guys, I have to take this."

She answered the phone as she strolled over to alleyway. "Hi, Mom."

"Oh great, you're still okay," Susan said sighing in relief.

"Why wouldn't I be?"

"I'm just not comfortable about you walking in the city like that without adult supervision."

Gwen strained herself from sounding exasperated. Yes, she was in the big, scary city; however, she wasn't nine years old anymore. Sometimes, it was hard for her mom to process that. "I'm fine, Mom, really, you don't have to call and check on me every two minutes."

"You never know what could happen sometimes, one in every two million kids get abducted."

"Geez, mom, are you trying to scare me?"

"Just giving you the facts, honey," Susan said simply. "Where is this place located?

"It's somewhere around Coney Island."

"Coney Island?! Good lord, that's a mile away."

"I'll text you once I get there," Gwen moaned, hoping this conversation would end.

"You get home real soon, honey. Real soon."

"Okay, Mom. I promise."

Gwen clicked off her phone, relieved to be released from the boundaries of her mother's worries. Once she made it to the alleyway to get some much-needed space, she saw two young girls leaning against the brick wall across from her. One had light blond hair, almost platinum, staring idly at her iPhone. She wore a rather tight-fitting tank top, emphasizing her bust, and low rider jeans. The other girl had a shimmer of light brown knitted up into bouffant long down her waist, wearing a low cut black dress too far from her knees with black fishnet stockings. The brunette girl was rudely smoking a cigarette at Gwen's direction, who tried to peel away from their attention, yet it was so hard to do. They made a very uncompromising duo.

"Hey, don't I know you from somewhere?" the blonde said, her green-blue eyes specked with interest.

"Um, no," Gwen replied, evasively. This girl *can't be* from Hamilton, but if so, it will be one more punch-to-the-gut of embarrassment for the day.

"I could've sworn I've seen you in Mrs. Sutter's class," the girl remembered.

Gwen, feeling defeated, gave up. "Yes, that was me," she said weakly. "I just got sort of lost within schedule, I don't really go to that class. it's my new year there, actually."

"Woah, small world. I didn't know this was your spot, too." The girl let out a giggle. Gwen was ready for whatever harsh comment this girl and her friend would retort but Gwen could see in her eyes that she was being genuinely friendly. "It's just that you don't seem like the type to…"

"I know. I'm doing study lessons with a friend."

"Study?" The girl laughed. "Who the hell would study *here?*"

"Yeah, well it was somebody else's suggestion."

"By the way, I'm Shawnie Jenkins." The blond girl giggled lightly. "I can just go on forever without saying my name. And this is Tara." She pointed to the brunette beside her, who dismissively pulled out a small bottle of gin from her purse.

"Tara, come on, aren't you over Ron?" Shawnie exclaimed.

"I need some time to grieve, okay," the brunette girl whined. "He was the longest boyfriend I had in six months. Oh and, hey."

Shawnie rolled her eyes, ignoring her. "She'll get over it," she told Gwen. "So where are you sitting?"

Gwen was surprised at the girl's eagerness to socialize. "You're coming with me?"

"Well, why not? I met you this far right?"

When they reached over to the patios, Shawnie stopped her tracks, her eyes enlivened with animation. She grabbed a hold of Gwen's arm, her fingers twiddling in her trenchcoat. "Is that Vera Hudgens?"

"Yea…Yeah," Gwen said, confused.

"Oh my gosh!" Shawnie squeaked. "I heard she's looking for an actress for her film, I have to talk to her! Tara, are you coming?"

Tara didn't respond. She was too busy, giving her studied attention to the biker boys around the block.

"Hmm. Never mind her, let's go," Shawnie said, pulling Gwen with her.

Shawnie raced across the patio for a chance to receive Vera's blessing. Gwen had never considered Vera to have some adoring fans in her circle. She thought of Vera as a low-key kind of girl who had a hidden talent, though not quite reaching the point of recognition. But having at least one admirer was enough measure to get herself noticed at school. However, Shawnie was different. Her vibe was not at all snobbish or even arrogant, not parading to get her face in the crowd. There was an impeccable innocence to her that she hasn't seen from most girls at Hamilton. She was very down-home, regular, an aura which Gwen felt comfortable in.

When the two girls made it to the patio, Shawnie was uncontrollably gushy. She pulled out her hand to shake Vera's. "I'm Shawnie Jenkins, nice to meet you."

Kyle leaned over to Gwen's ear. "Who is that?" she whispered.

"She's a student at our school," Gwen whispered back.

Kyle studied Shawnie's tight tank top and low rider jeans visibly showing a pink thong. "You've got to be kidding me."

"You have a very fine eye on the camera," Shawnie complimented.

Vera arched an eyebrow, incredulously. "You think so? Have you seen any of my work?"

Shawnie took a moment to recall. "Um...Yes. I was at one of your after-school film studies last year. You seemed very detailed in your line of filmmaking."

Kyle leaned into whisper in Gwen's ear, again. "I think she's lying."

"Thanks, I guess," Vera said, deciding not to press any questions. She wasn't sure if she remembered any beach blond girls in her first term film class.

"What I really wanted to talk to you about is being part of your film experience," Shawnie said, breathlessly hopeful. "I'll give you my best."

Vera broke into a wide grin, her brown eyes brightening. "That's great. Just come by next week at Central Park and I'll see how you do."

Shawnie jumped around the table gleefully and gave Vera a tight hug. "Thank you! I'll make you so proud!" Shawnie happily sat down, her butt in view of Kyle's direction, while she looked away in disgust. "Don't mind my prying but who's the male co-star?"

"David Henderson," Vera said matter-of-factly.

Kyle recoiled in surprise. "*The* David Henderson? You sure he can act?"

Vera combed her fingers through her hair, shrugging off Kyle's skepticism. "Well, he wrote a good poem that really fit the movie's tone, So I cast him."

Kyle disapprovingly smirked. "From what I've seen, Vera, the boy is a nervous wreck. I'm not sure if he's camera-ready."

"Enough with the criticizing, Ky. I know what I'm doing."

Gwen checked her watch. Her mom was probably waiting anxiously on the couch, having those pesky worried thoughts in her head. She didn't want the hour to go by any longer. It was around five-fifteen, so it was early enough to take the subway ride back home. Going on a subway train by **herself** was a risk she was willing to take. No matter how perturbed she was, she had to do it. It was all about inhabiting the soils of city life.

"Sorry, guys. My mom's waiting for me. I have to go," she said reluctantly. She would've liked to stay longer but staying past six o'clock would be a dent in her curfew. If she had one that early.

"Aw, I wish you could hang out longer," Vera said sweetly. "You seem really cool."

"I've only talked to you for a minute" Gwen said shyly.

"I can tell when a person is cool just by looking at them."

Gwen smiled. She thought she could never be the one to make friends easily. Though, somehow, these girls had come to trust her. Even Shawnie, by the look in her eye, took a liking to Gwen. Right now, at this moment, she felt really good about herself.

"Oh hey, I got an idea," Shawnie persuaded. "How about we all meet up at lunch tomorrow and get to know each other more? I know you guys have lots to talk about."

"That don't seem so bad," Vera agreed. "We'll form a little group session."

"I'll be there," Gwen shouted, crossing the down the street.

As she walked back towards the subway district, Gwen felt a calm discern of optimism. She might be a long away from her friends back home, missing every moment she had with them, but starting her life anew was a big challenge for her to take. For never-the- less, the path was slowly leading her to a new world of possibilities.

◆ ✳ ✳

TOGETHER AGAIN

Gwen woke up to the morning bells of the cathedral, having a good night's rest after her rather eventful evening yesterday. The subway ride back home was quite pleasant this time around. The evening train was less crowded and hostile, not too many people with short fuses or short time schedules. After catching a taxi ride from the Penn station, she instantly rushed home, and like an excited child, she told her mom everything. Cause who else would listen to her trials and tribulations at school than her dear 'ol mom.
Astoundingly, it didn't turn out depressing than she thought. She made a social group within one day, which was a miraculous achievement, so it was smooth sails on her second trip to Hamilton. Gwen ignored the constant stares, not caring about the glitzy dress code rule everyone seems to be consumed under. *Designer knock-offs, overrated.* Gwen felt much comfortable in a simple white t-shirt and blue rider jeans.

At lunch, Gwen expectantly sat with Kyle and Vera, as they gathered around for their planned meeting. The dynamic of the three girls were intangible. Kyle, the intellect, Vera, the liberal, and Shawnie, the optimist. As way of agreement, each girl decided to tell their individual life stories before their arrival at Hamilton.

First there was Kyle, originally from Mapleton, Rhode Island, a few miles from Providence. Her father, William, worked as a human studies professor at Brown University, and her mother, Patricia, was a former librarian turned psychologist. They were the kind of parents who wanted to raise their kids to be the next Einstein or Steinem. There was oldest Tom, who was on the debate team, served as class president, and eventually went to Harvard, currently in his junior year. Youngest Evelyn was an aspiring figure skater, utilizing her skills on the city skating rink on the weekends. Which left Kyle as the middle child of the family. At age ten, Kyle was able to read The Secret Power of Middle Children by Catherine Solomn, giving her the confidence needed to use more brain power when it came to school work. Patricia took note from her grand book of parental psychology, where in the last few chapters, it informed when children grow into adolescent stage, always encourage their strengths. What other skills did she had other than reading and researching? This was the time where Kyle needed some advice from her mother. Patricia, in her strict, annalist mode told her daughter, yes, that's what she was good at. It was good to know her skill set, but Kyle was in deep defeat. She wanted to be the type of girl to break out of the academic isolation she was living under and lead to greater heights. Though by her own accordance, Kyle continue to delve into her studies, fueling her determination. Her grades skyrocketed from the result. William, who went by philosophical terms, told her to always believe in deep thinking and be the best at her goals. And as a gift of appreciation, William gave her one of his published books: *The Study of Human Individuality.* Since arriving at Hamilton, Kyle wasn't at all fazed by the decadence of her catty classmates or the impeding drama around them, it was about getting even when it comes to using her high I.Q. to her advantage. Toying with their weaknesses on certain school subjects was just the reward to show off her academic prominence. If you can't join 'em, beat 'em.

Now, it was Vera's turn. Her parents would describe themselves as contemporary pop impressionists, the type of artist that could mold something simple like a piece of construction paper and a picture frame and turn it into something out of the ordinary. Her father, Lionel, was a sculpture enthusiast, who was the primary owner of Picasso Remedy, an exclusive nightclub for artists to meet other artists in the San Francisco underground. Her mother Melinda was an Iranian-born photojournalist, known for her eye-catching photos of the islands of the middle-east. By the time her older sister Matilda was born, Vera's parents ventured on to different projects. Lionel continued to do his sculpture work, being the talk of the town of many art galleries while Melinda switched careers as a yoga instructor. She spent most of her childhood in a picturesque suburban neighborhood in Seattle, Washington, the opposite of her parent's infrequent lifestyle.

It was at age twelve while lounging at home on a rainy day, Vera had the mild curiosity to peek in her parents' vault, which was the family basement. She was never allowed to go in there when she was younger, for who knows what kind of oddities her parents collected. Being home alone, she was able to unlock the mysteries behind that door.
Naked photos of Persian women and men were plastered on the wall, strange sculptures of the human anatomy were circled around the middle of the room, and just by the far-left corner was a box of videotapes. All fifteen were labeled with only three names: Warhol, Jodorowsky, and Deren. With divine instinct, she chose Deren. The film was titled Meshes of The Afternoon, and Vera was entranced by the visuals. Mesmerized by the fast editing and signature camera movements of the film, the experience was unsettling yet captivating. Once Vera came to know the name of Maya Deren, her inspiration was unleashed. Her first attempt behind the camera was making a short film during the summer before eighth grade called *The Origin of Flowers,* recounting the week to week blooming period of her mom's garden. It was hours spent on stop motion and still-capture, breaking away from any free time she barely had, but to her notion, it was worth it.

Upon hearing the announcement of her parents' move to Europe, Vera decided to go to New York City with her sister, who just so happens to drop out of college to join a rock band. It was a way to pursuit her dream of enrolling at NYC film school, fulfilling her wish of becoming a renowned artistic director. Although it wasn't as ideal as she perceived, living in a ramshacked apartment in Queens, with three unruly twenty-somethings, she mainly kept herself occupied to achieve her goals. Sure, the school she was going to wasn't her cup of tea, but she had just the amount of time and effort to serve her purpose in the city that never sleeps.

Then, lastly, there was Shawnie, blithely telling her tales of the California west coast with whimsical perception. Immersing into livid memories of lying face down on the sunny beaches where the surfer boys rolled by, beyond the blue waves of the ocean tides. Orange County was her pleasure dome, the place where you can feel free in your skin, but it was so many miles away now, her yearning to go back was still fresh in her mind. Her mom, Kathy, was formerly known as teen model Katrina, using her looks to get her way. Fearing her career could be over by the age of twenty-five, she enrolled at beauty school, although she had tried different methods to keep her finances afloat: Charming a guy with a huge wallet. Marriage upon marriage, prenup upon prenup, her total of weddings alone was a record of six. The alimony checks paved the way for Kathy to have her very own beauty salon, which expanded into a profitable business, given her short legacy in the fashion circuit. From the line of Kathy's many suitors, Shawnie had no clue who her father was. She was pretty sure she fingered out his name in the mail as she sneaked a glance at her mom's monthly checks, however, it never came to fruition. And in some doubt in her mind, she was afraid to ask her mom, because she refuse to waste her imagination upon a man she didn't know. By way of acceptance, she thought it was best to erase it from her memory. The time will come for her if she ever gets the chance to meet her father, but for now, she wanted to escape to the joys of her young teenage life.

There was a boast of jubilation once Shawnie remembered the last few days of her beloved golden state. She was going through the first stages of womanhood, eerily looking mature for her age. Therefore, upon her approaching that chronicle in her life, there was unexpected puppy love. As she basked underneath the sun on a clear mid-June sky, sitting on his high chair above her was a real definition of a man, or boy, she wasn't quite sure. He was just shy from eighteen, yet his appearance was mature and virile.
Shawnie was frivolously frolicking around with her childish friends, intimating Pamela Anderson when he caught her eye, this magnetic force pulling him to her. Shawnie was twirling around in giggles as she bumped into him. Looking up at his sandy brown hair, sharp gold-green eyes, and his exquisite jawline, the sparks flew instantly. He presented

himself as Derek, working as a lifeguard for the Malibu Makos surf club, to save up for Berkeley in the upcoming year. He had goals of being a marine biologist, usually discussing long topics of mammals living in the Arctic and Atlantic Ocean but Shawnie was too busy getting lost in his allure, not worn down by his boring attributes. She didn't tell Derek her age right away. She didn't even brag to her friends about him, knowing they were deemed one of those girls who could cause some sort of commotion by not keeping their mouths shut. Derek surmised that she was quite younger than expected, not a high school junior as assumed. However, the relationship continued.

They spent their nights under the moon, passionately making out. Shawnie was too scared to go all the way, and Derek didn't pressure, he was quite a gentleman about it. He also didn't treat her condescendingly when it came to her age, gaining the respect that she didn't get much from most boys her age. There was actual love, a love she thought she never could feel before or later. Through her romantic ecstasy, accordingly, she kept him like a dirty little secret. Older boys may be tantalizing but the pursuit of them was still scandalous. The day suddenly came once Kathy made the decision to expand upon her business and The Big Apple was just the place to take that leap. Shawnie tasted the tender lips of his kiss one last time, his muscled biceps wrapped around in her embrace. The break up was short and sweet, and so then, Derek went off to college. It was such a sad, miserable day for her. Not only she was whisked away from her high-end paradise, but also the one guy she thought was her true love.

At first, the city seemed aloof to her. Not at all the sunny, casual existence she knew in the bays of Orange County, yet, the fashionable jet-set lifestyle conjured her desires. During that year, she met her friend Tara, who was fresh out of Newark, New Jersey while making weekend getaways at Coney Island, and started dating a senior boy named Ian.

As a rite of passage, Shawnie decided to give up her virginity. Some part of her did like Ian, cute with his smooth athletic physique much like Derek's, and a bad boy rock star edge that made him one of the school's popular lacrosse players. Yes, he was certainly attractive enough, but he could never match Derek's tenderness and understanding. Off and away Ian went, going to a college in New Hampshire. This time it wasn't as heartbreaking because her body and soul wasn't in the relationship as she led on to be. But maybe, in that beacon of light, a boy, a special kind of boy, would sweep her off her feet.

In New York, you can always open your options.

It all came down to Gwen. There was hesitation. The girls had such unique lives, it was hard to compare. After all, if she cut out most of the drama surrounding it, her life was pretty mundane to the point where she didn't know who to tell it to. So, it went like this:

She was born in North Carolina, she had two best friends but didn't disclose them any further, and her mom's notoriety as journalist got her to where she was now. Plain and simple, nothing more, nothing less. The time of revelation had to come between the lines. But to her acknowledgment, the girls were genuinely fascinated. And as the hour went by, there was this immense attachment. These four girls were going to be stuck like glue.

At Vera's request, the girls took a taxi ride to lower east Manhattan where they settled at Caryle's, a popular hot spot for aspiring musicians. It had a beatnik, sort of jazz quality to it, the lights dimmed into a shadowy ambiance, surrounding in its mystery. A jazz band was playing on stage, strumming the melodies of an old Frank Sinatra song. Although the singer had an edge to her---hair striped with blue cut in an emo style, arms covered in tattoos---yet she was dressed in a purple flowered sundress to soften her presence. Once she belted out that old familiar song of *New York, New York,* There was a seductive growl in her voice, invoking her stimulation upon the audience.

The next song was Funny Valentines. Gwen closed her eyes, drifting into the lyrics of the song. Earlier in the day, she tried to spot the curly-haired boy at the library, but there was no sign of him. It was always like this for Gwen. A boy becoming eternally trapped in her romantic daydreams, never to be seen again in her reality. She remembered how his brown eyes smiled at her, the waves of his hair swift by the side. If only she could say two words to him. Two simple words...

Gwen shook out of her reverie, distracting herself by getting the girls some drinks at the bar. Once she got back to the table, Shawnie wasn't at her seat.

"Do you know where Shawnie is?" she asked the girls. Kyle pointed over to the crowd of people where Shawnie was engaging in a conversation with a shapely brunette. Gwen gazed at the girl with an ounce of familiarity, she could've sworn she seen her before. But as the girl turned around, her recognition instantly resurfaced. The girl's heart-shaped face was frozen in shock, her expressive blue eyes widening within sight.

"Gwennie?" the girl said in soft amazement.

"Max?"

The brunette jumped up in zestful elation, hugging Gwen tightly as she could. Gwen stood there in disbelief. Maxine was here. She was actually here, hugging her at this moment. Her manifestation of times lost, almost brought tears to her eyes, emerging but not quite coming down; she didn't want the reunion to be too emotional.

Maxine...was so different now, almost unrecognizable. Her soft round features were more longer and succulent, her body toned to perfection, and her skin tanned into an exotic golden glow. The length of her hair was more luscious, long down to her shoulder while the unimpeachable brightness of her baby blue eyes was now sharp, decorated in smoky eyeshadow. Her style of clothing was shamelessly ostentatious, wearing a glittery halter top with Juicy Couture jeans and an expensive pair of high heels, which Gwen assumed to be Christian Louboutins. Maturity can be a mystery sometimes. A woman, not a girl, was unfolding before Gwen's eyes.

"What are you doing here!" Gwen shrieked with delight.

"Well, long story short, my father's cookie business is freakin' booming. He just signed an expansion deal that netted seven million. Not to mention, I just had a sixteenth birthday!" Maxine boasted, swaying her luscious hair for the benefit of a group of boys crowded in front of her, their eyes following her every move.

"Oh my gosh, Happy birthday!"

"And you know what I asked my Daddy on my birthday, I said, 'Daddy, I want to go to New York.' And here I am."

Shawnie shifted between them. "Wait a minute, you two know each other?"

Gwen gradually wrapped her arms around her old friend from Statesville. "This is Maxine. One of my friends from North Carolina."

Shawnie's eyes were star-struck. " *You're* Maxine *?* How awesome!"

Gwen cordially stepped away giving the girls some much needed alone time. They somehow complimented each other to which Maxine was feeding into Shawnie's gullible admiration of her. Maxine never outwardly portrayed a sense of confidence but that exuberance she so desperately wanted to display, had come to her calling.

As Gwen walked ahead over to the pool table section, A biker girl came into the entrance door. She had jet black hair styled in a bob, ala Joan Jett, wearing a leather jacket decorated in rhinestone under a white tight tank top-jeans ensemble. She strutted along the place, adducing a command in her presence. The biker girl then slyly leaned in between two young guys playing pool, tapping one of them on the shoulder, gesturing for a cigarette. The guy suavely pulled out a Marlboro while gazing at her hungrily, slowly placing a cigarette between her fingers. The girl nodded her head and casually walked off as the two guys continue to gawk at her.

The sting of strange familiarity came back to Gwen. Whether the girl was meant to bring attention to herself or just so happen to stop by at the place, she couldn't escape the feeling she seen her before. Not a school or anywhere else for that matter, but from a distant reminiscence, fitting in piece by piece.

Just for curiosity's sake, she followed the girl. She thought it was weird of her to do so but the connection was too strong in her mind to clear it out. The girl stopped at an alleyway, a back-door light illuminating her. Gwen felt awkward standing beside the girl, quietly watching her take each draw from her cigarette. The girl vaguely noticed Gwen, and not one for starting conversations, she braced herself for a proper introduction.

"Hi," Gwen said in a quick shrill.

"Uh, hi," the girl replied, confused. She quizzically turned towards Gwen, squinting her eyes under her dark thick bangs. Then her eyes grew wide.

Gwen looked at the girl more clearly. "Mona?"

"Gwen? What the fuck?!" Mona shouted jovially as she enveloped Gwen in a bear hug.

"I thought I wasn't going to see you in about a couple months," Gwen said almost out of breath. "How did you get here?"

Mona's smile slightly faded. "It's a long story."

"It's the sweetest thing you came because Maxine's inside. You wanna come see her."

"I...I don't know."

Gwen was taken aback by Mona's dismissive reaction. It was inevitable. Gwen had to play peacemaker yet again. The go around between Mona's stubbornness and Maxine's bluntness, it was bound to be difficult. Although it wasn't an easy job, at least she could teach the girls the meaning of mutual understanding.

"You don't seem that excited," she said, hopelessly.

"It's not what you think," Mona solemnly explained to Gwen's relief. "Something happened back home...Maxine only reminded me of that. Not that I'm blaming her. I mostly blame myself...I just wanted to get away." From all the years Gwen spent with her, Mona harbored a defeatist attitude masked under a tough exterior, hiding the lost little girl inside.

Gwen wrapped her arm around Mona's shoulder. "What did happen, Mona?"

Mona inhaled slowly. "It's, uh...It's going to take a while, I'll probably have to start from scratch."

The bad timing of Mona's conception put a steep restriction on her parents' future. Emma was barely sixteen when she had her, and just as Art was finishing up his senior year and preparing for college, time stripped him away from seeing Mona's birth. But their courtship didn't happen out of inconvenience, they were very much in love with each other, though bringing a baby into the world had been a scary experience for both.

Art left for Appalachian State University by the end of the summer, leaving Emma with most of the burden of parenthood. There were relatives close by, though help was scarce. After the long-distance setbacks and Art's apathy towards Mona, the relationship begin to falter. But two years of growing maturity led the couple to salvage their courtship.

When Mona was just five years old, they got hitched in a simple, private ceremony. One half of Art's family members, along with Emma's tempestuous mother, Barbra, thought it was a horrible idea, predicting the marriage wouldn't last long. They were, in fact, correct. After four years of traveling difficult paths in each other's lives, they filed for divorce. During the separation, Emma completed her degree in nursing and signed on to medical school while Art focused heavily on his construction business. Emma decided to continue her medical career at the Kingsbrook center at Crown Heights, a neighborhood in Brooklyn.

It was one of the biggest sacrifices Emma had to make to build a life for herself and Mona, as New York was a better opportunity for her chosen career as an OBGYN. And in her intuition, she thought it would also be a chance for Mona and her dad to be closer, however distant he came off to be. Emma promised a teary-eyed Mona she'd make a home for both of them, as her and her father stood at the bus station. And, just like that, Mona looked far off into the distance as the greyhound bus drove away, clear of sight.

Mona's preteen years wasn't the best. She felt emotionally isolated due to her father spending so much time with his construction business than building what was left of their relationship. Going away on his supposed business trips, Art would leave Mona to relatives or to the demands of her grandma, Barbara, not-so-affectionately known as the Barb. One minute, she was the typical fun-loving "cool" grandma, though not a moment too soon, she would lash out at the most inconvenient things. This was the usual bouts of her bipolar disorder, and by refusing to take her daily medication, it caused her to have irritable tantrum fits. It was no mystery where Mona's stubborn nature came from. The toxic mixture of Barb's painkillers and weight loss pills made her mental effect even worse.

Mona consciously blocked out the verbal threats and name-calling, but it was too hard to erase it. It was one incident, a devastating verbal attack that struck Mona to the core. Her own grandmother called her a mistake. At just ten years old, she didn't know how to make of that. Why would her own grandmother say such a thing? Looking back on it now, Mona knew Barb wasn't herself, however, those cruel words disillusioned her. So much so, she almost believed it. Whenever her mom came to visit, Mona ran to her loving arms, to keep her safe, to keep her from whatever emotional pain she was concealing. Her father felt resentment of their close bond, grounding himself with more ambition, never really taking the time to acknowledge his daughter's plea for his understanding.

As the years went on, progressively into her teens, Mona became more sullen. Inhabiting a rebellious streak of diving into a sea of sex, drugs, and rock 'n' roll to hide her detriment. Gwen was the only one that kept her on solid ground, to not lose her path to self-destruction. Gwen was someone she can count on in her time of need when there was nobody else to turn to. So, when she saw her friend, all packed up and moved away by early-June, Mona felt deserted and alone. Maxine could be considered a friend...when she wanted to. Mona thought of her as weak-minded, willing to do anything to schmooze with the in-crowd at Statesville high, that the word 'doormat' was labeled on Maxine's forehead. One day, she was unusually eager to invite Mona to an upcoming birthday party Kelly Tennant was throwing. She was one of Amber Krecther's so-called friends, the kind of cheerleader who would send out cookies for charity. Mona was genuinely surprised. She'd rather be caught dead than join the escapades of the popular crowd, but she accepted the invitation, even if she was looked upon as Maxine's tag- along. It was soon to be one of the biggest mistakes of her life.

The party went smoothly at first, however, once the copious amount of alcohol, marijuana, and over-the-counter prescription pills came into the mix, the mediocre social gathering became the rowdiest parties Kelly has ever thrown. Mona, living on the edge of impulse, found herself making out with a guy, going into a room, and reveling in uncontrollable lust. The next week after that, she had no idea what was in store for her. The name-calling, the gossiping, the snickering all rolled up into devious stares watching her every move. The hostility surrounding her classmates confused Mona until it hit her. She'd slept with Evan Meyers, Kelly Tennant's boyfriend. It was obvious Amber was her main target by spreading malicious rumors, but this one happened to be true.

Kelly, who was usually upbeat and non-confrontational, was easily swept into the vicious cycle, thanks to Amber's coaxing. Evan had cheated on her plenty of times without knowing, but Kelly being the dutiful girlfriend was so oblivious and up in the air, she couldn't read it from a mile away. Therefore, when Mona's name came out of her friends' mouths, yes, oh yes, Mona was always at fault. Amber and the girls even went so far as to bring up the rumor about her making out with Laci Fowler. Her sexuality was sacred to her but since that came out unceremoniously, her alleged promiscuity in tow, led Mona further into more ridicule. Maxine did nothing to help. How could she? She was trapped under the watchful eyes of Amber, like a dog on a leash. How could her father help? He was barely there to understand what she was going through. There was only one solution: leave town.

So finally fed up with all the grieving, Mona got up the nerve to call her mom. Taking the early morning train, she had a reflection of what she would leave behind, erasing it as soon as the train pulled off. By the time of her arrival, Mona was surprised to find her mom newly engaged to a man named Alfred, a co-worker at Kingsbrook and saw that the home was just the right fit for her. She no longer felt the oppression of her ill-fated hometown.

Gwen held Mona's hand. "Gosh, Mona. I wish could've stuck by you."

Mona squeezed her hand back. "What could you do? The situation was out of control to the point where, even though I left, the emotional scars are still there."

"That's why it's good that you're telling me all this," Gwen said, uplifting the conversation. "To let your feelings out. Which is why I keep a personal dairy of mine. You should have one, too."

"Well, Gwen, I'm not particularly the type of girl to be writing in a dairy," Mona jokingly retorted. "I got my good o'l uncle Ray's guitar for that."

"Exactly! That's even better! So are you coming inside?"

Mona hesitated, turning her head away.

"There are some people I want you to meet," Gwen said playfully, putting on a puppy dog face, with her hands clasping together on the side of her cheek.

Mona broke into a small grin. "Sure, Why not?"

The two girls went inside where they found Kyle, Vera, Shawnie, and Maxine, sitting at a table near the far end. Mona slowly walked up to the table with a dead serious look on her face, her green eyes, fierce as a leopard, staring directly at Maxine. At first, Maxine was unsure who Mona was at first, but once her recollection came to her, the relaxed expression on her face went stone cold. Gwen felt the tension rising between the girls, Mona shooting invisible rays at Maxine, who was willing to take on her any challenge beset to her.

"Uh, hi, everybody, I would like you all to meet Mona," Gwen introduced. The girls waved awkwardly, oblivious of the situation at hand.

"Mona, it's nice to see you," Maxine said, smiling through her hidden anxiety. "I can't believe you're here. Must be a small world isn't it? I never thought New York would be an easy city to get to, considering we came at the same time. You, me, Gwen, together again. It'll be just like old times..."

Mona put her hand up to stop Maxine from rambling. "Before I have this little reunion, I want to get some things off my chest."

Maxine had her mouth shut, her eyes wide. Gwen and Mona took their seats. Mona took two breaths and had her hands placed on the table. All eyes were on her, but she focused her attention on Maxine.

"I know we had some rough patches," Mona began. "And I know we both can be real pain in the ass, but I want to forget the whole Amber Krecther drama. There was nothing you could do. You were practically her slave. No offense."

Maxine raised an eyebrow, amused at Mona's assumption. "I wasn't her slave, I was her confidant. I just didn't want to be involved in her bullcrap. If I said one word that defended your character, she'd have me on her shit list, fair and square. She's the mayor's daughter for christsakes."

"Beside the point," Mona proceeded, waving her off. "I don't blame you. I want to let bygones be bygones and see how things go from here. After all, we need to grow and learn from our mistakes."

The tension in Maxine's shoulders dropped and she went back into her cool, calm self. Gwen let out a sigh of relief, so did the other girls.

"Well, to hell with Amber Krecther," Maxine said perkily. "What I have is a new lease on life and that's how I see fit."

"You haven't said it any better," Mona said with an approving nod.

Vera sprinted from the table and stood proudly in front of the girls. "Since we got that out of the way, let's introduce our new comrades to the big red apple," she said, raising a drink to do the honors. "Now repeat after me, 'to a new life and new city.'"

"To a new life and new city," the group recited in unison.

The girls regressed back into their social gathering. Mona was now in a much lighter mood, talking openly and freely, pulling all the weight off her. It was exhilarating to let things go, especially with people who actually listened. With old friends and new friends, the three musketeers were now made of six.

THE CITY OF DREAMS

Maxine Triffendorf awoke from her slumber, feeling the soft, silky fabric sheets of her canopy. She inhaled in ecstasy. She was finally here. The great, grand New York City, paving her way for miracles to come.

When the moment her father, Gregory, signed a business deal with Yorkshire, Maxine had a speck of hope that her life was going to change forever. She gazed at her reflection in the rose-pink vanity mirror, pursing her lips in satisfaction. Her efforts of altering her appearance over the summer had remarkably succeeded. Fitting in with the socialites of the Upper East Side wouldn't be a problem at all.

She traced her eyes around the room, taking in the beautiful scenery. Every time Maxine set foot in the incredibly affluent penthouse, a deep impact of euphoria soared into her soul. The inside of the living room was like a grand palace, the walls decorated in rich vanilla alongside a golden tile floor, shining like the gold halo around the sun. The bedrooms were painted individual colors. Her parents got boring brown striped with blue, their furniture fancy enough for a typical middle-aged couple, however, Gregory and Leigh-Ann interior taste was akin to their rather dated view of nineteen-sixties counterculture. Maxine was relieved to oversee her own décor, and it was just the way she wanted it. Everything was painted luscious pink, a little girly but still sexy. There was a glass door to the balcony, and a grand canopy bed in the center of the room. Just how she envisioned it. Then there was the living room, where French white sofas were prepped in front a massive pine wood coffee table and a fireplace below a Victorian painting by Albert Lynch. Her dream house has finally been restored into its mastery.

Looking back, the move from Georgia to North Carolina was headache-inducing. It started when her father's cookie business began to dwindle after the economic crash, forcing the family to relocate for better business prospects. What better choice than some backwoods, middle of nowhere town like Statesville. She knew her dad was broke but he wasn't that "broke." At least her mom and dad were able to move into a quaint, middle-class neighborhood, not apart from its nosy neighbors but the environment was nice enough. However, going to school was excruciating and humiliating. What she hated most about her first day of school, was how her mom would give her these weird designer clothes shipped from Europe around the time of her stay in Georgia. Leigh-Ann was still in contact with the stylist her great aunt Sylvia suggested, this cutting-edge French extraordinaire, who was experimenting his chops on kids' outfits. Wanting to go cheap on her savings, she thought it was a neat idea to ship his samples for Maxine to try on, all the while endorsing the rest of the money toward her upcoming cosmetics line.

The style was a mix between Kogal, a well-known Japanese fashion trend, and nineteen-sixties fashion wear, with little hats and bows included. Leigh-Ann's favorite TV show was *That Girl,* obsessing over the outfit Anne-Marie wore in the opening sequence. So, she thought it was a splendid idea to dress Maxine in a similar outfit on her first day of school. The kids just stared at her in complete confusion. She just looked so out of place and abnormal, dressed like an oversized baby doll with a plump face and wide figure, that the kids were cruel to her since day one. Fat Charlotte was the nickname they gave her, causing her to spend days in a river of tears. When the kids heard stories of her wealthy background, the casual taunting leveled up into envious disdain. Till this day it was hard for her to comprehend her orchestration for having an upscale upbringing, but ten-year-olds were always jealous of anything. Maxine finally found solace in the welcoming arms of Gwen and Mona, who kindly gave her acceptance despite the flaws she presumed she had.

Middle school was a lot easier. By gaining a bit of confidence and changing her diet, she managed to succeed her social status and kept up with the latest trends. The benefit of puberty also helped, losing all of her baby fat. And now, she was even old enough to choose her own wardrobe. During the summer before ninth grade, she even wrote a special list to get through her first year in high school:

1. Wear all the latest fashions by top designers

2. Walk with grace and confidence

3. Show your million-dollar smile

4. Hypnotize your admirers with your spellbinding personality

Following those simple rules got Maxine on the right path. Every night she would practice talking in the mirror, fluctuating an eloquence to her strong Southern accent. She wasn't embarrassed by it by any means, she just thought her twang could add a little more spice to her growing maturity. Her final step to completing her path into girl- womanhood was to learn how to walk in heels. The test wasn't as bad as she expected it to be. Head up, back straight, and strut your way. She had it at the palm of her hand. But there was one obstacle from keeping Maxine to climb the ladder of social reign: Amber Krecther.

With her curtain of long blond hair draped down her shoulders, lustful sea green eyes, and long legs like a gazelle, there was no match for her, really. From the first three weeks, she already had recruited two comrades. Funny how Miss Straight Lace was willing to put a stamp on her newfound territory: A public high school located in Hicksville, North Carolina. This Amber girl was quite the charmer. Captivating boys with her gorgeous looks while mesmerizing the girls with her cool, casual demeanor, Amber took her popularity status at ease. Amber knew how to play the game and she played it just right. Hell, Mrs. Amber Krechter, Mrs. Wannabe Queen of Them All, probably had more money than her, going through her daily rituals of weekend trips to the mall, wearing outfits fresh off the racks of Bloomingdales'. But as it turned out, Amber was, in fact, the town mayor's daughter. Therefore, Maxine had no other choice than to kiss her ass. It was the only chance to receive just some quantity of a high-end social life. It was totally beneath her. But why not, at least she got noticed, eventually becoming part of a clique. Not exactly true friends on her part but strictly a clique, nothing more or nothing less. Maxine eventually got along with the other two girls, Kelli and Tori. For the most part, they were nice and amiable, a bit bland but tolerable. It was hard to see that Kelli and Tori weren't on the same level as Amber, who took her reign on school grounds a bit too seriously. Whenever Miss Amber Krecther stomped her heels down the hallway with tyrannical prowess, Maxine, Kelli, and Tori would trail side by side, being branded as mean girls by association. As cliché as that may be, it was just society's dense view of high school culture.

Kelli was a cheerleader (of course) but not at all stereotypical. She was positive, optimistic, and rather sincere. Tori was more studious, though not without exposing her wild reputation on their nights out. But the two girls were wrapped around Amber Krecther's toxic influence, leading them to the dark side.

Maxine never knew she had such willpower. In any case, she never thought girls like her even existed. Living a life like that, playing the cards with every deck towards a target at each hand was too much to handle. But it wasn't about having the power, it was how to handle that power. How to put anyone under your spell, charm your way out of anything, and put someone in their place. It was addictive; it was invigorating. Maxine wanted that so badly. But at the same time, it was about having fun, fitting in, living life to the fullest, painting every picture of every moment in the last few years of childhood.
Fulfilling those wishes was endearing to her. Although there was one thing Amber Krecther did taught her, is that whether people will adore or hate you, all you have to do is flip your hair and strut your catwalk. That's all it took in the popularity game. Too bad Amber's reign didn't last that long, thanks to her father's recklessness. Down, Down, she goes into her quiet little shell by the countryside, her once bourgeois decadence came crashing into a muddy grave. And so at last, Amber was never seen again. Poor Amber

Krecther. Whatever happened to her? Who cares. It was all about playing the social gamble. Betting and betting until you got it just right. The risks her dear father, Gregory, took was just as similar. He had spent years building his great-grandfather's name, purchasing the rights to his long-forgotten product, kick-starting the Bakersville cookie factory after his death. With the help of Donald, her beloved granpappy, they raked in investors and lawyers to build up the Bakersville family business into an industry, transferring from North Carolina to the sweet nectar of Manhattan. Gone were the days of making out with boys on the back of rusting pick-up trucks, the embarrassing infomercials of her mom's faltering cosmetic line, and being a lackey in someone's place. This was *her* time to shine. A time to be smart. To be elegant. To play by her own rules.

Maxine stared out over the balcony; elated satisfaction caroused through her veins. This was her utopia.

New York City...

◆ ✳ ✳

J. D. Fitzgerald

EXAMINING THE ART OF FILMMAKING

Vera Hudgens sat at the front row of the classroom, tapping the heel of her Doc Martens nervously. It was Tuesday at film production and editing class, where each of the students were assigned to turn in their short film admissions. Every school year, Mr. Buford would start the course with a five-minute short film homework lesson. Vera wouldn't expect any of her classmates to be masters of the camera eye. After all, their five minutes of short films consisted of walks in the park, sightseeing at times square, and a tour of the museum. No matter how uncommitted they were by sheer laziness, half of her classmates always had a ninety-percent chance of getting a passing grade. She spent a whole week of her life working on this supposed "masterpiece," though in the back of her mind, she still felt it wasn't good enough. For the occasion, she had watered down her look: A dark blue turtleneck and a black pair of slacks, her usually spiked hair was parted neatly to the side. Now if only her classmates would take her a little seriously, she wouldn't be as skeptical. But how could the students of Hamilton Academy take anything seriously? There were some who cared about education and world culture, though most of the population of Hamilton are filled with careless nitwits who rather spend their mommy and daddy's money on a new Lexus. Those were the ones that were sitting here in this classroom. They weren't what you call the 'artsy' types, their minds wavered into their frivolous hormones instead, living life with everything handed to them. But it was Bianca Walworth, the critic of speculation, sitting like a queen waiting for approval, while her two- gal pals were in for the kill. The peach-haired one made an exaggerated yawn to prove their point. Vera could feel them, staring from behind, far from the last row. *What do they know about film, anyway?* She wasn't there to impress them; she made the film that she liked and that was that. As she would describe the almighty Bianca's short film, it was the recreation of the nightclub scene in *Casablanca*, filmed at the Waldorf-Astoria with her lovey, dovey Chace. It actually had high production values, considering her boyfriend's connection to the Hollywood scene. It was such bullshit how Bianca would shove her relationship into people's faces, declaring her love for this guy when in actuality, he seemed suffocated. How amusing life is to be surrounded by spoiled rich kids with nothing to do.

As if by serendipity, Vera discovered Hamilton on the Internet while searching for schools to transfer to at the start of her sophomore year. It did have its perks, serving classes that were fresh on the curriculum. When she read about film production and editing class, her eyes lit up. On the manual, the description read, whoever had a chance to pass the class would have a greater chance to receive a scholarship to NYCU. Vera had to make a brave decision. It was either a boarding school in London or enroll at a school with the hopes of exploring her artistic prowess at the NYCU Tisch School of Arts. Hamilton was the definite choice. How lucky she had been to put film production and editing into her schedule.

Vera had a rough patch adjusting to the school on her first day, unfortunately. Since this was an influential private school, Vera had to make a good first impression. Upon her suggestion, she decided to cut off the dreads she styled the year prior for a smart, appropriate look. Vera did make the mistake of cutting her hair a wee bit too short and wound up with an unfortunate bowl cut. She tried to coax Matilda and one of her bandmates to help her repair the damage, but it was no use. She walked inside the school with a super short Caesar haircut. In her French class, one of the junior girls made a snooty remark at the teacher.

"Why is there an eleven-year-boy in the classroom?" she quipped as the kids yowled with laughter.

Vera hid her face in the books, to single herself out for most of the period.

She felt so out of touch within the environment of the school, separated from its strict, manual social norms. Vera wasn't sure where she can fit in. In the following week, as a way to get involved in extracurricular activities, Vera signed herself in for the school newspaper. Although she had no interest in journalism, Vera eventually got along well with the other staff members. Being bored by the standard news articles, Vera and her newly found confidant, junior editor Roslyn Gruber, developed an idea to add to the newspaper platform, an art magazine titled *Titan.* The magazine didn't take off like she wanted to but at least it was an outlet for the Hamilton misfits, forming a steady community. In over two months, Vera was finally confident enough to lead a social group inclined to her radical agenda, therefore, making her more than welcome to put her place within the halls of Hamilton.

The movie brightly illuminated the screen. The title appeared in blood-red font, slowly disappearing into the scene. Vera's name flashed in bold letters, making sure to remind everyone *she* was the director of this movie. She named the short film *Every Dead Rose Bloom.* Quick cuts of films and commercials merged together. Clouds floating by in fast motion. A man giving a red rose as a cherished gift to his girlfriend. A white rose slowly disintegrating into a burnt crisp. White doves flying towards the blue skies in slow motion. Then Vera's most excellent work of art came into play.

A beautiful landscape of Central Park, panning over the trees rustling and the flowers glowing in the bushes. The camera slowly went up into the summer sky, flashing into the ray of light, transitioning into another scene where a drop of blood spilled upon the same withering decrepit white rose, turning it back into its beautiful form. By sleepless weekends of editing, Vera knew in her heart the scene was praiseworthy.

After the film ended, there was no applause or no faces in deep wonder. Just complete silence and snickers. Vera knew this wasn't her type of audience.

"Thank you, Vera, for that interesting showcase," Mr. Buford said in his low, tedious tone. Beneath his rather blasé response, he was actually impressed, as he was a former film critic at the *LA* Times, known to be an avid fan of Avant Garde directors such as Derek Jurman. From the first day she enrolled, he knew Vera was a secret visionary talent. Considering his love for the arts, he would often challenge his students by way of stiffed expression. Unlike her pupils, Vera studied the signs of body language. Whenever Mr. Buford was satisfied with a project, he arched his eyebrow. Whenever he disproved, he twitched a frown. He raised both his eyebrows by the end of the presentation, thus granting Vera the seal of approval.

Finally, the bell rang, sending the kids running out free from their dolorous classroom.

"Vera, can I speak to you for a moment?" Mr. Buford called after her.

Vera stood at his desk while he sat authoritatively in his chair, smiling admiringly.

"That was an astonishing piece of work, Vera. Very descriptive," Mr. Buford said ponderously. "Tell me, what was the message behind the story?"

Vera broke into a clever grin. "May I sit down with you, sir?"

Vera sat down at one of the auditorium chairs in the front row beside him, her legs crossed in a poised manner. "The whole concept is the state of the world, confide by its destructive division and reckless abandonment of our political climate. The earth is full of trees and flowers, *we* are like trees and flowers. And then there's the dove, which symbolizes rebirth, resuscitation of a better nation."

Mr. Buford nodded his head, intently. "You're a bright girl, Vera. Now be sure to work hard at turning your goals into reality. You have a tremendous talent. Use it well."

"Thanks for the advice, Mr. B."

The road to NYCU was two steps away. Beyond the coming of senior year, Vera was bound to take command. Passing this class was a piece of cake. Now she had to think of her next game plan, starting the pre-production of her upcoming short film, *At Love's Lost.* She had her male lead already...She just needed to convince him to play the part.

There he was, standing at his locker where she would always find him...David Henderson. On one of the first few days at Hamilton, she had met him, sitting alone at a lunch table outside, reading the poems of John Keats. He was wearing a large black hoodie under a skinny frame, the hood flipped over to cover his face. Vera had been relieved she wasn't the only weirdo at school. *At least, I look more normal than him*, she'd thought.

It started off as an awkward conversation, both of them saying one word at a time.

"Hi."

"How are you?"

"Fine."

"Nice haircut."

"Thanks, I guess."

He spoke in a low, gentle voice, soft yet masculine. It was hard to see some of his facial features under the hood of his jacket. But as he lifted his head, Vera saw a twinkle of honey brown in his eyes hiding underneath ringlets of curly red hair. He was so adorable it made Vera's heart melt.

Vera persuaded him to join her art club, but he declined. He wasn't exactly a people person despite being at Hamilton for over two years in the wake of his junior year. Although it took time for him to open up, he eventually warmed to Vera once she got on the subject of her film interests and showing samples of her short films, thus beginning their friendship. David was also friends with Zeke, who've known each other since middle school. During spring break, the three of them went on a train ride to the Hillside Cafe. Vera took this opportunity to pull David aside and reveal the choked-up feelings she had for him. She had a sort of crush, something that she's been itching to get out for a long time. So, she made her move. Standing across from the pier, she was alone with him. Without saying anything, she kissed him hard on the lips, holding it for a few seconds. When she broke away and opened her eyes, there was a bewildered look on David's face. And she knew why. There had been no fireworks. No passion. Just a quick peck on the lips. Suddenly, her view of him had changed. It was amusing how she would longingly fawn over David when she came to realize there was no spark to be had. The memory of kissing David was like kissing her big brother. It was all too weird. Maybe Vera had been desperate at the time though, after all, he wasn't anything like the boys at Hamilton.

Right now, David and Vera had a close platonic relationship and nothing out of the norm. But from then on, they were two lost souls of the upper east side.

Feeling a rush of anticipation, Vera walked up to David. He had no acting experience whatsoever, but it was now or never. David was the romantic manifestation of the wounded knight—this could make or break her film.

"David?"

"Yeah?" David replied, blinking his eyes in attention.

"I was wondering..." Vera took a deep breath, "if you could be the male lead in my short film."

Vera said it all in one sentence; it took David a while to sort it out in his head. "Okay, I guess."

Vera, full of relief and joy, jumped into David's arms. "Oh, thank you. Okay, stop by at Carlye's after school, we'll discuss the scenes and protocols there. You're a life saver, man."

Vera raced down the hallway, leaving David standing at his locker, flabbergasted.

Everything was set, and all Vera could smell was roses. This artistic venture was going to be her finest. Poetic, sentimental, and sensual.

There was one thing missing, however...The perfect Natasha.

68

J. D. Fitzgerald

◆ * *

COLD EMPTY HOUSE

Bianca stared at the white marble walls, weary of the quiet stillness of the dining room. She was having one of her depressing so-called family dinners. Eight-thirty on Wednesdays was the only given quality time Bianca has ever had with her parents. Mom would have her board meetings and Dad would have his client meetings. Yet whenever family affairs were involved, Bianca always had a desolated perception.

Her father, Neal Walworth, was one of the most respected lawyers in the New York judicial system. He was an Ivy league graduate who soon ranked up his status to run his own law firm. In the courtroom, Neal was known to be a master manipulator, trapping every witness through his intense cross-examination. Eroding his power over the courtroom, he would have this command in his voice, giving everyone his direct attention. He had that strange effect on people, this strict authoritative man who'd use his steel-gray eyes to lead the way. He kept his workplace flourishing, hiring each willing participant to unlock the world of cooperate America. Running a successful law firm stripped most of Neal's attention away. Bianca, who so desperately craved for his approval, pressured herself to be the daughter he wanted her to be. But here she was, sitting at the table with an apathetic man who cared more about his career than his own family.

Her mom, Marla, was the daughter of Count Peter Yusupov, member of the Russian nobility and Vivian Saunders, a former ballerina. Through her mother's connection to the fashion industry, Marla, at age eighteen, got a gig at the Ford modeling agency. Eluding the captivating elegance of Grace Kelly, she soon made her stance on the runway while garnishing her skills as a fashion designer. By age thirty, Marla had a successful run as senior editor of *Vogue*, eventually funding her own fashion empire.
Couture was one of the most top-selling fashion magazines on the market, prompting Marla to take hold of the business with an iron fist. She was always a woman in control, only showing emotion when pressed to. Occasional visits at the metropolitan and annual fashion events was the only mother-daughter bonding she had with Bianca. Marla was anything but the overbearing stage mom, forcing her to wear the latest fashions hot off the pages of her magazine. Marla craved beauty and perfection, living vicariously through her daughter's youth. Bianca felt like a mannequin on display. It was all too weird, and it was all too fake, how each of her mom's colleagues fawned over her,

concealing their ulterior motives. She had plenty of opportunities to be on the pages of *Couture*, but she declined, refusing to be Marla's puppet.

Neal squinted his eyes at the newspaper, vehemently. "Damn son of a bitch. He nailed that last case."

Marla primed up her blond bob, and took a drag off her cigarillo, uninterested in her husband's expertise. "Don't worry, darling. I'm sure there is a big court case waiting out there for you."

"My honor society group is planning this fundraiser for the endangered dolphins in Japan," Bianca announced, breaking into the conversation.

"That's great, dear," Marla said brusquely, running her fingers through her hair.

Neal took another scan of the newspaper, turning the other page. "You know the Bernstein Company is accused of withholding fifty percent of their company's share. I might just get a lawsuit from one of the employees. Whoever wrote this article is a one fine intellectual, very detailed in her facts. Maybe I should invite this reporter for our luncheon next week," he boomed excitedly with a satisfied chuckle.

Bianca stared down at her food. It was a fine meal of smoked salmon, romaine lettuce, and lemon fried rice. She only ate half of it. They always did this; waved her off like a pestering child. Did she even matter to them? Was she important enough? She was their daughter, heir to their legacy; they should appreciate her more than they did.

Bianca put her fork down and pulled herself from the table. "May I be excused?"

"As you wish, dear," Marla said absently.

Bianca made her way up the marble stairs and into the long corridor. By the left side of the hallway, she reached the china cabinet, containing some of her dad's collection of liquor bottles. She chose the white wine, drinking from the bottle to feel the smooth taste of green grape sizzling down her throat, all of her pre-expectations melted away.

The taste of wine gave her immense relaxation. It calmed her, soothing out the endless migraine of her brain. Eliminating all the demands of school, popularity, and after-school projects. She just wanted to escape, escape somewhere to ease her mind. She placed the bottle back in its spot and closed the cabinet door.

When she entered the bedroom, the first thing Bianca gazed upon was a golden music box...A gift from her beloved grandmother, Vivian. She opened the box, listening to the soft tinkling of *Swan Lake,* the toy ballerina spinning to the melody. She pulled out a pack of French cigarillos and took a drag. She laid down on the Egyptian threaded quilt, letting all the memories sink in.

Countess Vivian Saunders was a woman who lived her life and lived it well. Funny how she didn't carry the frosty demeanor of her daughter Marla. Vivian was soft and eloquent in her approach yet carefree, always letting her long hair down. Watching the little toy ballerina twirling in delight, revitalized Bianca's memory of her grandmother, capturing the glory days of childhood.

Now widowed, living alone in her four-bedroom Gothic home in Connecticut, Vivian preferred not to have cable, choosing to watch recordings of long-canceled shows such as *E! True Hollywood story, Mysteries and Scandals* and *Intimate Portrait.* She would entertain Bianca by telling stories of her days as a rising ballerina star while staying at a boarding school in Switzerland. During concert shows between New York and Los Angeles, she got invited to the wildest celebrity parties, getting familiar with the well-known stars of the golden age. But it was her arrival at Russia where she met a young aristocrat named Peter. She was soon to be married into Russian nobility at age twenty-four, during the peak of her career. Although she had an abrupt early retirement, she kept most of her memorabilia as keepsakes. Photos, costumes, and a fifty-year old projector were all kept in her study room. A five-year-old Bianca would glow in wonder, seeing how her grandmother, strawberry hair long to her waist, gliding flawlessly across the stage with every twist and turn in sharp swift movements in the running film. Spending those precious summer days, experiencing the magic of history's long past, was the most treasured moments of her lifetime. Bianca remembered it all. Vivian was the one who brought life into her. Even in her older years, she always had that exuberant, youthful spirit. So many Sunday afternoons, it had been the two of them, watching old movies and sipping homemade iced tea at the backyard patio. Those were the years of solace.

Then in an instant, it all changed. As time went by, as people got older, a tragedy could strike in the most surprising of ways. When Bianca turned fourteen, she heard about Vivian's cancer.

The days in the hospital room were excruciating, seeing Vivian deteriorating before her. Vivian's luscious strawberry blond hair was graying and thinning, her dazzling violet eyes grew sunken and dull, and her already thin body was emaciated.

On the last day she'd seen her, Bianca laid her head to Vivian chest, hearing the beating of her weak heart. She'd cried uncontrollably, tears falling down her face. She never wanted to let go. Vivian quietly soothed and hushed her. Her last words were, "Be the best you can be and don't let anybody stand in your way. I will always love you, my little angel. Be strong."

Her funeral was on a rainy day, the raindrops pounding heavily on her casket. She forgot what it felt like to lose a loved one. The pain was sharp and slow, clawing at her inner soul.

Bianca kept her eyes on the ceiling, the tinkling of the music box pressing softly in her heart. She took another drag from her cigarillo, letting the tears flow gently down her cheeks. She held on to the amethyst ring her grandmother had given her.

Then the music box stopped.

◆ * *

A VERY HOSTILE MAKEOVER

Gwen lounged comfortably in the living room couch, watching episodes of Adventure Time on her DVR. It was a lazy Saturday afternoon and all she wanted to do was relax and eat Chinese food. Susan decided to work an extra day, leaving Gwen the apartment all to herself. She stared out the window, still entranced by the glass skyscrapers. It would be nice to explore the depths of the city, get lost in her surroundings, though it could be better to stay at home and enjoy her free weekend, safe in her own personal cocoon.

Just then, there was a buzz on the intercom. Gwen rushed to it and pressed it in. Who the hell would come by this early in the day?

"Hello?"

"Hey, girl, ready for some afternoon shopping?"

"Max?"

"Yep, it's me. Now are you going to let me in or what?"

When Maxine entered the door, she was all dolled up in a tight mini dress decorated in red and orange stripes under a dark blue denim jacket. Shawnie trailed along after, getting back to her more risqué clothing by wearing a yellow smiley-face T-shirt, showing her midriff and a short plaid skirt, her legs laced with black fishnet stockings.

Maxine slowly walked around Gwen, examining her like a test subject.

"What?" Gwen snapped, trying to hold back her annoyance.

Maxine touched her chin with the tip of her finger, eerily like her mom would do. "You need a makeover for sure."

Gwen scoffed in amusement, walking to the refrigerator to grab a bottle of water, as if brushing off Maxine's silly suggestion.

"What I mean is, it's time for a change," Maxine announced.

Gwen plopped on the couch and sighed dismissively. "What is there to change?"

Maxine walked closer to her, her face softening. "Gwen, honey, look at yourself. You're still wearing Hello Kitty pajamas. Don't you think it's time to grow up? Change your style up a little?"

Gwen just sat there with a blank stare, then thought about it. From the look of things, nobody took her seriously. Here she was, this mousy little girl lost in the pathway between childhood and adulthood, too afraid to show her true self. Maybe a little touch up wouldn't be such a bad thing. She did yearn for a change and yes, she wanted to look more grown up. "I guess."

"Okay then. The third and most important rule in my personal handbook, is to have a marvelous smile. So, let's start by getting rid of those god-awful braces."

Gwen eyes widened in alarm. "No way. Mom would kill me."

"Oh stop worrying, Gwennie. She probably wanted to get rid of those braces a long damn time ago," Maxine assumed dismissively. "You had those suckers for about three years already. Now come on, girl. We got a long day ahead of us."

Sitting on the couch, Gwen picked at her braces, expecting sharp pains through her teeth when Maxine came near them. Was this even going to work? She could feel the wires tightening up the crowns.

Shawnie hopped up and down, clutching her purse in exhilaration. "Oh, this is going to be fun!"

Maxine pulled out a pair of pliers and a screwdriver from her shopping bag and marched right up to Gwen. She could feel the cold blood flowing inside her. Maxine was totally not kidding. She really was going to rip the braces off of her.

Shawnie held Gwen's hand and gently whispered, "Breathe in, breathe out."

Maxine kneeled in front of Gwen, staring hard at her teeth. "Wow, I have to be honest with you, I'm not a dentist. And I don't know what the hell I'm doing. But this has to be done for your sake."

She plowed the screwdriver into Gwen's mouth, picking at the loose wires, making it wider. Gwen sucked back the drool building up from under her tongue, which was wiggling wildly left and right. The wires slid off like a piece of thread between her teeth. Not an ounce of pain at all. Gwen blinked her eyes open. Maxine stared at the pliers in her hand; the remains of the wires were dropped on the floor. She held up an oval mirror to Gwen's face to show the results. Her eyes grew wide. Her teeth were completely crystal-white straight.

Maxine snapped the mirror closed with a satisfied smile. "Mission accomplished. Let's go shopping, girls!"

Gwen quickly dressed in a plain white T-shirt and a simple pair of jeans as the girls made their way to the elevator. Maxine frowned at her grungy appearance while idly searching for a variety of clothing stores on her phone. As she followed them exiting the sliding doors, Gwen's mouth dropped. She was standing right in front of a white stretch limo, the rims of the vehicle jeweled in crystal clear diamonds. Oh, what a day this was going to be.

"Woah, look at the size of that! That's your limo?" Gwen said in amazement.

"Well, duh. I told you, I'm worth about seven mil and plenty more. In my humble opinion, limos are pretty cheap," Maxine said vainly.

"I couldn't believe it, either." Shawnie beamed. "I am so siked!"

Inside the limo, Gwen leaned lazily against the window. Out of the comfort of her home and into the streets of Madison Avenue, the reality of being here still puzzled her. Today was the busiest New York has ever been. Watching the crowd of pedestrians colliding in the sidewalks, the ray of sunshine contrasted into a blue haze, and the rows of buildings passing through each time. The view was invigorating, like riding through a dream she couldn't wake up from.

The limo parked at the Barney's department store, not long after. Gwen's stomach dropped once she gazed up at the big, fancy store in front of her. She was hesitant to come in, but Maxine pulled her along, her high heels clicking at a zippy pace.

A whiff of lavender and lemon balm savored the entrance area. The sounds of a baroque symphony played over the intercom. Racks upon racks of lavishly expensive clothes were decorated in gold, silver, and lame'. Each section of the store was branded boldly with the top designer brands: Versace, Dior, Armani.

A middle-aged woman, dressed in a black turtleneck and black slacks, came to greet the girls with a smile. "What can I do for you, ladies?" the woman asked politely, even as she gave a questioning glance at Gwen's clothes.

"We need a makeover for this girl, care to show us the latest outings? Maybe a clearance sale we can check out?" Maxine asked persuasively.

"Sure. Right this way."

While the girls went off on a tour, it gave Gwen more time to browse the store's surroundings herself. Gwen observed the lavish garments on display. So specific in the clothes it sold, she imagined how silly she'd looked in them. She wasn't sure if the color palate on the fabric would match her faded complexion. Though she wondered if she ever been at retail store this huge, so established in its style of decadence. And to Gwen's surprise, there was an elevator on the other side. She had the urge to at least try it out. She had ridden in elevators before but every time she did, she would hyperventilate, due to her fear of heights. But maybe it would be different this time. Riding in the glass elevator, overseeing the store's structure miraculously eased her worries.

When she entered the building, it was just racks and racks of more clothes by designers she didn't know. Racks of name-brand shoes she could hardly pronounce. It was all too new to her, walking into aisles of the abundantly sumptuous clothing store the girls at her school were so used to.

Behind the dress rack, Gwen begin to hear a group of young female voices talking on the other side.

"Do you really think this dress suits me?" one girl said in a soft, almost somber voice.

"Of course, it does. The clothes you wear always has a classic touch," another girl said, her voice casually blasé.

Gwen tiptoed around the racks, peeking through the clothes.

"Why don't you wear some of the dresses from your mom's magazine? You can get it for free, right?" a third girl said in a voice that was airier, more chipper than the other girls.

"That's out of the question. Being the daughter of Marla Walworth is a basis of irony itself. You think I wanna try on clothes from every Couture issue she publishes? I'm setting up this party on *my* terms."

"But it might give you exposure," the breathy-voiced girl continued. "I mean, you do have a better fashion sense than Rain Bosworth."

Gwen stumbled back, knocking over the rack. She got up from the floor shaking in panic. The three girls turned around. The one standing in the center stared at Gwen quizzically. She recognized the fierce cat eyes, the raven hair, the imposing regal appearance. It was Bianca Walworth, who was not happy to see Gwen invading her turf.

"You've got to be fucking kidding me," Bianca said venomously.

Gwen took two steps back and started dashing for it. She could hear the sound of laughter as she rushed off, her heart pounding intensively.

Gwen crouched against the corner of the elevator. *How do I belong here?* she thought. She felt like such a fish out of water, being in this part of New York where beauty, importance, and style mattered so very much. The cool kids' content with their maturity and grace, privileged by royalty. Gwen was never even born from old money, making it impossibly far-fetched of her to join in such a lifestyle. What change would come out of this makeover? How could she prove herself by wearing clothes she didn't even seem to like? As Gwen slouched off the elevator, Maxine intercepted with four bags in her hands.

"Gwen, where were you? I've been looking everywhere," she said, tapping her heel. "Come on, we've got a lot more to do."

"Where are we going now?"

"Next stop, Katrina's," Shawnie said confidently. "My mom owns the place."

Going to a place called the meat-packing district didn't really appeal to Gwen at first, but as the girls strolled down the neighborhood, the place was larger than life, crafted into a trendy New York hot spot. They made their way to a building across the street from One Jackson Square at one-twenty-two Greenwich ave. A bright pink K was implanted above the main doors of the stone-gray exterior. Faint sounds of island music played in the background and as the girls went inside. It was like stepping into an otherworldly tropical wonderland. Tall palm trees towered on each corner, the bright lights reflecting the mirrors glowed like the western sun, and the wallpaper was painted sky blue striped with a warm orange color.

The store's owner, Kathy, was dressed up in a tye-dye shirt knotted up to her midriff with daisy dukes and red pumped heels. Not particularly the type of clothes a typical mom would wear. Her blond hair was hoisted up into a messy bun, giving her an exuberant youthful appearance, though there was evidence of Botox filler from the stretched tightening of her cheeks.

She greeted the girls kindly, showing off her pearly white teeth. "Well, Shawnie, it looks like you made some new friends."

"Mom, I would like you to meet Maxine and Gwen. Gwen, here, wants to update her look. Got any suggestions?"

"Oh sure. Come over here, sweetie," Kathy perked up, prepping Gwen in one of her steel chairs. She stared into the mirror, concentrating on Gwen's features, turning her head left and right. "A little layering must do."

"How about we make her blond?" Maxine offered.

Gwen made a stink face. "Blond? I don't know."

"Gwen, trust us," Maxine soothed. "It'll bring out your eyes more."

Shawnie gently rubbed Gwen's shoulders and cooed, "Just close your eyes and think of something nice."

Gwen closed her eyes, listening to the Caribbean beats of island music playing on the radio. The crashing of the waves, the cawing of the eagles, the whistling of the summer breeze, reminded her of the last days she'd spent with her father at Wilmington beach. The view of the faraway ocean crashed into her memory. The images of the lucid dream ran through her mind further until she heard Shawnie's voice breathing in her ear. "Open your eyes."

Gwen opened one eye, giving a slight peek. Then once she opened both eyes, Gwen took a deep short breath. She couldn't believe what she was seeing in front of the mirror. "Is that me?"

"Oh yeah, sugar, it's all you." Maxine clapped her hand excitedly. "So, what do you think?"

"I'm speechless," Gwen said breathlessly.

Maxine proudly put her arm around Shawnie's shoulder. "Well, ladies, our work here is done."

Coming back from the limo ride home, Gwen braced herself for her mother's reaction as she tiptoed from the living room to the dining room.

Susan was just on her way to the kitchen when she got home from work. Gwen held her breath, standing behind the door. Susan's back was turned, busying herself by making espresso. And just as she turned to face Gwen, she steadied her tracks, her eyes widened in surprise.

"Wow, Gwen, what did you do to yourself?"

"Hi, Mom."

◆ * *

BRAND NEW CHICK

It was the early dawn of eight-am. Gwen quietly sat still in the cab, waiting for the inevitable. She was feeling fidgety with the outfit she had on today, not sure if she could flaunt it off. Last night, during the ride home, Maxine gave her a makeup kit, followed by a pamphlet of instructions. Step one: apply makeup. Step two: apply outfit. Gwen, for the first time in her life, learned the basics of makeup foundation. The colors blended well with her skin complexion, though she couldn't help but worry that there were girls who probably looked ten times better than she did.

Gwen was so torn. She could skip out now if she wanted to, but she had to face her fears somehow. She stared ahead; the school building was at a far distance. Her heart skipped a beat.

"Gwen, honey, are you going to get out of the cab?" Susan said, tapping her shoulder.

Gwen blinked her eyes. "Oh yeah, s...sure."

"You think you can walk in those heels? They're kind of tight around ankles there."

"I'll manage," Gwen said assuredly. "I've been practicing since this morning."

After bidding her mother goodbye, Gwen stood before the school. She wasn't sure she had ever worn heels at all. She almost stumbled in the effort of climbing up the steps, the pointed ends of the shoes clamping in the concrete. These were black leather boots that were too mature and too high for her to stand. When she entered, Gwen expected all eyes on her as she slowly walked through the crowded hallway. But from what she observed, there were not looks of disdain, but more of an intrigued puzzlement. To her wonder and everybody else's, she finally evolved. Her stringy brownish dishwater hair was now streaked sunshine gold, full and silky. She was dressed in a Vivienne Westwood ensemble: a hot pink mini dress high above the knee and a cropped black jacket. She knew at any given moment, nobody would recognize her at a second glance, which was a good thing. The stares became more apparent. Gwen continue to look straight ahead, avoiding any sudden eye contact. A sense of unease was propelling her, her left hand quivering as she held on to her book bag. Maybe today wasn't going to be as smooth as she thought.

Later at lunch, after wading through gasps and whispers, Gwen sought refuge at the table where Maxine and Shawnie were waiting expectantly. By the time Vera arrived, Gwen anticipated her reaction.

"So, what do you think?" Gwen asked uncertainly. "Too revealing?"

"I must say, Gwen, you did an upgrade!" Vera exclaimed. "A very dramatic change in wardrobe."

"Well, I guess our handiwork is a success after all. Isn't that right, Shawnie?" Maxine bragged.

"Oh yes, totally," Shawnie beamed.

Gwen pulled down the tight dress. "I don't think I can handle this."

"It's all about being comfortable in your skin," Maxine informed. "My most important lesson in my personal rule book, is to have a spellbinding personality, and that, my dear friend, is always the key."

Bursting through the cafeteria doors, a girl with crimson shoulder-length hair grabbed everyone's attention. Her outfit was smart and sleek paired in a tank top, a blazer hemmed to the waist, and slacks matched all in black. Though by the look of her surly expression, she didn't exactly embrace the confident exterior of her appearance.

The girl casually sidled up to the table. "Happy now?" she sharply retorted to Maxine. "I must look ridiculous."

Gwen slightly squinted, seeing if there was a sting of recognition. The girl brushed off her fire-colored bangs and looked at Gwen quizzically. She suddenly recognized the steely emerald eyes. Yep, it was definitely Kyle, and she looked positively stunning.

"They got you, too," Gwen said simply.

Kyle rolled her eyes, smoothing out the outline of her jacket. "Well what choice did I have? These two practically ambushed me after school."

"So how did it go?" Gwen asked.

"We were able to track her at the library, 'cause the girl *loves* to study, and just so you know, we caught her in our little web of reconstruction." Maxine clasped her hands together like a diabolical mastermind, feeling mighty proud of herself.

"I vehemently refused," Kyle filled in. "But with a lot of forcefulness…and suggestions, I gave in eventually."

"Oh, stop that fuss," Maxine said in a cavalier manner. "You look damn good, and you know it. You're in the fashion capital of America, honey. You can't just go walking around the school dressed up like a grandma."

Kyle scoffed. "I happen to be comfortable with the way I dress." She got out her physics book, blocking out the conversation entirely. Gwen knew it would take some time on Kyle's part. She promised herself to never be on Bianca Walworth's level of beauty standards, although right now, she was wearing a designer knockoff, delving into temptation. It appears Maxine and Shawnie didn't have to try too hard to comply with Kyle. She knew she wanted to be a part of the crowd. Who wouldn't? It was of importance to any girl at any school whether public or private. Kyle was just too headstrong to admit it.

For Gwen, it was a new beginning. *Whatever happens* was her motto for the moment.

Gwen caught herself staring at Bianca's intense violet eyes. Just one foot away from her lunch table, Gwen felt a sharp feeling in her spine as if it been struck by lightning. She expected hatred behind Bianca's absorption, yet instead, it was a look of confusion, surging at her with the unasked question, "Who's that girl?"

Someone else set their eyes on her. A familiar pair of midnight blues. Chace Fairbanks was practically marveling. All Gwen could do was smile nervously. To be sure, his girlfriend was sitting RIGHT next to him, so it wouldn't be wise to reciprocate his obvious attraction to her. Bianca worriedly looked at Chace, who reacted by looking away, embarrassed. Then she gave Gwen an instant stare. This time, a look of envy.

Once the bell rang, Gwen inhaled a breath of relief, not wanting to be caught in a tug-of-war. Chace Arlington was ogling at her. Actually ogling at her in front of his girlfriend, making this day even crazier than normal. After waving her friends goodbye, Gwen merged in with the crowd of people out in the hallway; she didn't sense Chace standing behind her as she turned around.

"Hi," she said in surprise.

Chace made a sly smile. "Hi. You're new here, aren't you?"

"Two weeks ago." Gwen giggled shyly.

Chace leaned against the wall and gave this sort of sexy grin, those magnetic blues gazing at her. Gwen's cheeks grew redder. "What's your name?"

"Gwen...Gwen Stevenson."

Chace let out his handshake. She grasped his hand, feeling a warm sensation boiling in her insides. "Chace Fairbanks."

"I know," Gwen said breathlessly.

"Do you wanna talk sometime?"

"Talk as in go out?"

Chace nervously chuckled. "No, not exactly."

Gwen should be flattered that Chace was even speaking to her, but then she blinked. All she could picture was the envious face of Bianca Walworth. She took a step back. "Listen, I don't think I'm comfortable even being friends with you. I mean what would your girlfriend think?"

"Um..."

The awkward silence put a dent in the conversation.

Gwen looked at the floor, ashamed of even falling for it. "I'm going to be late."

She left him without a word, realizing what he had been trying to do. She wasn't going be played a fool. Just because she had this new, mature look, didn't mean she was going to use those assets to cause a breakup. It was almost disgusting. She was actually going to go along with that, losing some part of her consciousness by letting things go up in the air. Chace was smooth and direct with his personal goal. He just didn't care. Gwen replayed Kyle's words, "Never fall for the charms of Chace Fairbanks" And that was very well true.

Chace wasn't the only one to worry about; it was everyone else, including the almighty Bianca Walworth. It was predictable to think that of her but how else would she feel? How would she feel about all of this? Nobody knew who she was, but nobody knew before. Her life was changing. Maybe a little *too* fast.

88

BLUE EYED SERENITY

Chace Fairbanks lazily laid his head on the grass, taking a drag from his joint. The marijuana made his body numb and his eyes blurrier. He threw away the joint, deciding he'd rather enjoy his shot of whiskey instead.

He was lounging at Central Park with his best friends, Jeremy, Austin, and Kenny. The senior boys would usually hang out at the sheep meadow after school, doing their male bonding ritual of playing football, smoking hash, and talking about future college plans.

Today, Chace definitely had something on his mind. He thought about how he should lead on legacy after legacy when he didn't have any interest in it. He thought about being the jack of all trades, Yale graduate–future stockbroker, but he really didn't strive for it. But most of all, He couldn't stop thinking about the girl who had eyes, the color of ocean blue. Chace was completely entranced when he approached her, he just couldn't help himself. What blocked his hazy vision was the hurt, angry face of Bianca, which added guilt to his regret. That's when he asked Kenny for another joint cigarette, having stayed in the shade for too long, he stepped out as the harsh sun put a sting in his eyes.

"Dude, what's in this stuff?" Chace said, his voice straining.

Kenny took a drag on his cigarette. "Natural California blend." He gave a friendly pat on Chace's back. "Think good thoughts when you smoke, man."

Chace followed Kenny to the meadow, propping up against the large tree by the shade. Jeremy and Austin decided to take a break from playing football and jogged along to the hillside.

Jeremy Flecther was the traditional blond-haired jock. With his height being a great advantage for him. Standing at around six'four, Jeremy was essentially one of Hamilton's hottest star athletes. He had just the right stamina to harbor swift athletic skills, to which Chace thought, he was the better choice for captain of the swim team.

Austin Caruso, who came from a prominent Greek-Italian family, was the noted wisecracker of the group. He had the ingredients of being dark and handsome but not quite tall, standing at only five'six. Most of the girls towered over him but he made up for it by showing off his impeccable charm...and washboard abs. Either the girls were amused or enticed. Usually both.

Kenny Osborne was the art prodigy. Being brought up from a biracial background, he was the perfect gentleman, exuding a laid-back, friendly disposition. Kenny worked heavily into his art projects to where his signature landscapes was featured yearly on the school yearbook. On the weekends, He'd go sightseeing at the museum by day and hang out at the Blue Note Jazz club near west 3rd by night. Half of his wardrobe consisted of nineteen-fifties inspired suits, having known to be much more fashion-forward than his group of friends.

On this very spot, they would often sit and discuss about their various interests, like how the girls would do in their little secret hideouts. But since they were men amongst men, their interests were typical of the male psyche. Today's topic was their favorite: girls.

"Okay, gentlemen, what special ladies do you have in mind?" Austin started off.

Jeremy sat back, stretching his muscled arm. "I got my eye on this redhead. She's kind of bookish, sort of the hot librarian type. But you know what they say about the quiet ones, bro."

"My special lady-in-waiting is this sassy brunette named Maxine. She's new at the school, which makes it all the worthwhile." Austin took a drag on his cigarette and gazed up at the sky in afterthought. "Kenny? Got any ladies by your side lately?"

"No rush. I'm kind of waiting for the right girl to come along," Kenny said matter-of-factly.

"Give it up, man. There are plenty of girls who would dig a cool jazz cat like you," Austin persuaded. "You know, chivalry is your best weapon."

Then the guys focused on Chace. He was extremely quiet throughout their whole conversation, his hands buried deep into his pockets. The subject of girls was a tricky subject on his part, considering his devotion to Bianca. But as his inner desires overreached his libido, the sudden thought of other girls entering his mind was heading for a deep impact. The periodical stress of final exams, college, and promises he'd never keep was at a short distance of time, slowly slipping from his grasp. To hell with it. He wanted to spend his final school year without any consequences.

Letting his thoughts roll by, Chace decided to change the subject. "So, you guys figured out what school you're going to?"

"Alfred," Kenny announced.

"Columbia," Austin said after.

"Ohio state," Jeremy said last.

"Well, I hate to break it to you fellas, but I have no clue where the hell I'm going," Chace said as he took a swig of his liquor bottle.

"Dude, you got Yale stamped at the back of your hand," Kenny reassured.

"The possibilities are endless, but Yale isn't one of 'em."

Chace looked out at the lush green lawn surrounding the red maple acres. He knew that the prospects of his future were in limbo. His friends knew what goals they wanted, knew what to accomplish in life, but the pressures from his dad to become the next golden boy of Wall Street was a heavy anchor on him. He just wasn't cut out for it.

The boys all circled around Chace, conjoining their hands together in the form of a group hug, their heads bowed in unity.

"Okay, listen up," Kenneth consoled. "No matter where we go in life, we'll always be brothers."

This was going to be the last few moments they spent together. From here on out, they were going to be living different lives, in different cities. Chace's own livelihood was tested, confided in a deep ball of frustration and confusion. The pressures of solidarity with his family dynasty was stifling, not sure if he was able to reach the same success, not sure if he was able to gain the same level of power and integrity his father has.

He was unfortunately listless with no clue of who he wanted to be.

J. D. Fitzgerald

ONE UNFORGETTABLE NIGHT

Bianca sat at the Plaza hotel Palm Court, sipping on a glass of Chardonnay. Nerves and excitement coursed through her veins. Tonight was her night. She was finally going to become a woman. She closed her eyes, imaging herself soaring in a cloud full of ecstasy...and pain. She took another sip of Chardonnay. The negative thoughts kept piercing with every daydream that flowed through her head. It wouldn't be all that painful, right? But Bianca had to think of a way to turn this into a positive experience. This was about her and Chace exploring each other in ways they haven't yet reached. She was bound to make this moment a treasure in memory. She prepared herself, planning and organizing as always, and even writing down a list. But first and foremost, she knew that putting a dramatic touch in makeup can always spark the flame, courtesy of her Dita von Teese beauty book. By flaunting her much mature, saucy appearance, she got a free drink at the bar, but not without a few name drops or two.

What immensely annoyed her was how everybody fawned over that new girl yesterday. But to her astonishment, with a slight squint of an eye, it was the same sad, baby-faced girl she kept seeing at the cafeteria, lavished in a sexy get-up. Just how did she afford those clothes, those boots, that purse? It was impossible. Fascinating that a girl of her stature can possess the cunning trick of the mind. And to think she was on scholarship. How tragic.

What really bothered her, though, was that Chace couldn't stop staring at her. Every once in a blue moon, Chace would sneak a glance at a girl. Bianca didn't want to come across as the typical jealous girlfriend, so she overlooked it. But the way he looked at this girl, this spark in his eye that seemed to waver, was beginning to be troublesome.

However, she brushed it off. She wasn't going to let this girl be a threat. She and Chace had been together for three years, nobody was going to ruin that. Certainly not after tonight. Speaking of which, it was minutes away from his arrival. She finished her drink, checked into her room, and loosened her trench coat for the sexy special peek.

While lit candles flickered and the smooth saxophone sounds of Astrud Gilberto and Stan Getz played on the radio, Bianca heavenly immersed in the silk red sheets of the bed. There were two knocks on the door. Yes, just on time. When the door creaked open, she rose up from the bed and opened her coat, waiting for Chace's reaction.

He stood there for a moment, in awe of Bianca's body through her skimpy lingerie.

She stretched her arms out in an eloquent pose. "Well, aren't you going to frisk me?" Bianca said in her best Breathless Mahoney impression.

Chace had his head down for a moment. "Bianca...Can we just, talk for a moment."

Bianca sat up on the edge of the bed, confused by the offer but obliged. "Sure, honey."

Chace sighed. "I don't think Yale is for me."

"Oh Chace, sweetie, I never meant to pressure you," Bianca assured him. "I just thought that's what our parents wanted."

"Bianca...there's something else I want to tell you."

"It's okay, tell me."

Chace took his time. "...I think we should see other people."

Bianca went pale. The words felt like sharp pins stabbing at her heart, in and out. She let out a breath, hoping to say a word. What came out was only, "Why?"

"Because it'll give us time to think more," Chace explained.

Bianca briskly sprinted up from the bed, fascinating her trench coat tightly. "What is there to think about?"

"I just feel like we're drifting into different crossroads in our lives. I don't know if I'm able to take care of you like I should."

Tears welled in Bianca's eyes. She let out a tender sob, her arms folded against her shoulders in disbelief. "This moment, this moment that should happen right now, could bring us closer together."

"I don't know if I'm ready, Bianca. And I don't think you are, either." Chace looked away. "I'm not the perfect boyfriend you want me to be."

"So, you want me to point it out for you?" Bianca whimpered, trying to hold back emotion. "Okay...You're irresponsible, stubborn, and incompetent. How's that for imperfect?"

The room got quiet. Chace let the words sink in.

Bianca knew him more than anybody, even more than his own friends. She wasn't holding back. She wanted to clear out the cloud of his seemingly perfect facade. And it felt good. It felt so good to just tell it in her own words, cutting deeply and slowly. But the walls were breaking down. They were no longer the sweethearts of Hamilton Academy. They were just strangers now, no longer hiding who they truly were or how they feel. Yes, the truth always hurt, and Chace indeed deserved every bit of pain beset upon him.

Bianca walked over to the mini bar and poured herself a glass of champagne, feeling the cold citrus sizzled down her throat. "I think you should leave."

Without saying a word, Chace headed to the door, solemnly taking one step after the other.

Fresh tears rolled down Bianca's cheeks. There was no way she was going to let Chace see her this way. Three years down the drain. Though maybe it was growing up, growing out of a high-school fantasy of what should have been. It wasn't the end of the world; however, it wasn't an easy pill to swallow. This was all about starting over. She'd lost her parents' appreciation, lost the one woman who was her only true friend, and now she lost Chace, the love of her life.

There wasn't much left for her. Nothing else to lose.

J. D. Fitzgerald

THE ODD GIRL OUT

Mona Margulies strummed the strings of her guitar, disengaging the screams of her mom's voice. Just like her good o'l uncle Ray used to say, "There's nothing like music therapy to get you through the day."

She guessed running away was an act of rebellion her father couldn't take, so Emily stepped into her defense. At first, the discussion was civil. Though the tension still lingered, it didn't come close to being blown out of proportion. Then the disagreements came and their bitter tangents of each other spoiled their reconciliation.

Mona put on her headphones and continued playing on her guitar, blocking out the painful memories of her childhood. Now that she thought about it, she was relieved her parents weren't together anymore.

There was a knock on the door. Alfred, her mom's fiancé, came into the room.

"How you are doing there, kiddo," Alfred asked in his thick Jewish accent.

Mona smiled at his concern. "I'm doing alright, Al. Thanks for checking."

Alfred was a mild-mannered bespectacled man, conservative yet sensitive in his own way, being the attentive father figure she never thought she had all those years. Only to have known him for about a week or so, Alfred gave her the sense of security she always wanted.

"It is intense down there. You sure your mom is handling it, okay?"

"They've always had their fights," Mona said exasperatedly. "It's nothing new."

Alfred sat on the bed and gently patted Mona on the back. "Well, just to cool things down, I got some good news."

"What's the good news?"

"Your mom and I had a talk with Susan Stevenson the other day and I think we may have found the right school for you. And seeing how you're good friends with her daughter, you might want to check it out."

Mona felt unsure but went along with it. "I don't see why not. When's the occasion?"

Mona entered the cafeteria, searching for the right table to sit at. It was like being surrounded by a pack of wolves, eyes following her every move. She had no idea what she was doing here. This school was so...abstract, if that's how she wanted to describe it. Shallow. Hallow. Transparent. At least in her mind.

So here she was, the great, grand Hamilton Academy from the Upper East Side. With Mona's sense of style and lack of etiquette, she had no idea how this could work out for her.

At least they didn't know who she was. Knew her name. Knew her secrets. A clean slate was what she needed. Having a reputation was hard to come by and wiping out all of the mistakes she made in the past was a healing process. Therefore, she needed to be closer to her mom in this time of need, to have guidance and support for once in her life. If she hadn't run out of town, it would've been worse from than before. She was glad to have Gwen at her side to get through the growing pains, however this school might turn out to be. But there had to be someone else to join in for the ride. And perhaps that someone was Vera Hudgens.

Mona signaled a wave. "Hey," she said with a sigh of relief as she sat at the table. "It's good seeing you here".

"Right back at you," Vera said with a snap of her fingers. "How do you like Hamilton so far?"

"Can't find the words. Weird? I guess? They sure like to stare a lot." Mona noticed she was wearing her "Misfits" T-shirt and a pair of torn black jeans for her first day of school. A simple outfit like that wasn't giving any praises.

"You're fresh meat," Vera explained. "You'd be the main course if you're some celebrity's kid or a loser who happened to have a trust fund, but they'll get used to you. let's say, in a month or two, the fresh meat status will wear thin quicker than you expect. So don't worry, I got your back."

From the sound of it, guidance was what Mona yearned for. She was a girl hanging by a thread, so ruled by her impulses that fueled her emotions. There were some regrets. She wished she'd never slept with Evan Meyers. Although he was a serial Casanova and Mona wasn't the only girl he was fooling around with behind Kelly's back, he had a certain charm about him and really nice six-pack abs. She had to admit, he was easy on the eyes. Mona was a victim of her desires, but it wasn't worth getting ridiculed for it. The kiss with Laci was actually something real and passionate. The fact of the matter is, she *felt* something with her, more than anybody she'd known. Laci Fowler was new at Statesville and was a star player on Mona's basketball team. It was friendship...that turned into something more. Laci was honest, optimistic, and understanding to Mona's plight, serving her as a devoted confidante. It all led up to the incident in the locker room.
Nothing was the same after that. Laci's parents were Christian conservatives. Once they caught wind of the story, they pulled her out of the school, sending her away to South Dakota not long after.

Mona suffered through grief and heartache, changing herself, indulging herself, just to numb the pain. Her only regret about that was...she should've fought harder. Been a lot stronger in supporting the relationship, but that never came to be.

She didn't know if moving to New York would be any better but a change in location was the only game plan she could think of. It made her hardships a lot less distressing.

"What brings you here?" Vera asked curiously.

"I don't know," Mona responded as she sank into her chair with depressive sigh. "Last chance, I guess?"

"It's not anything compared to having to wake up at six-thirty in the morning for a thirty-minute bus ride to deal with this Upper East Side bullshit."

"Thirty minutes?"

"Yeah. Being a New Yorker is brutal, especially when you're a teenager."

In the meantime, Maxine came strolling in with Gwen at her side. The expression on her face was that of a wounded animal, feeling not quite comfortable in her new clothes. It appears Maxine was primping her up like some European supermodel, clothed in a cheetah skirt and a white blouse. Maxine, being her normal attention-seeking self, was putting an insane amount of pressure on Gwen. What was her purpose in Maxine's quest for popularity? Mona even felt sorry for that annoying Valley girl who was following Maxine around like an emotional crutch.

Gwen smiled graciously and headed straight for the table as Mona pulled out an empty chair. When she settled down, Maxine cleared her throat. "Gwen, would you mind sitting with us at the other table?"

Mona struck Maxine with a look of death.

Gwen gave her a confused look. "I'd rather sit here."

"Well, if you wanna change tables later, be my guest," Maxine said slyly.

"Same goes for you. I know who my friends are, Maxine," Gwen said confidently.

Mona allowed herself a victorious smirk. Though she forgave Maxine for her past indiscretions, her shallow behavior was still intact.

"Suit yourself," Maxine said with a fake perky smile.

As the two girls walked on, the blonde turned her head and mouthed, "I'll sit with you guys tomorrow." Reminding Mona, that she could at least give props to the blond bimbo.

"Just your standard social climber," Vera quipped. "She is going to be the perfect ass-kisser one day."

"Fuck standards," Mona said sourly. "Just when you think somebody's changed, it's only to benefit them for their only selfishness."

Vera patted Mona's hand. "Oh, that is very true, my friend."

Mona placed her hand firmly in the center of the table. "From now on, we can only trust ourselves and the people we're close to, but not the ones who keep their distance from us. Agreed?"

Gwen placed her hand on top of Mona's, so did Vera. "Agreed," the girls said in unison.

Even though everything wasn't what it used to be, Mona kept her pride. Hopefully, that was enough to see wherever the crossroads may take her.

J. D. Fitzgerald

MAXINE TRIFFENDORF AT YOUR SERVICE

Maxine haughtily walked over to her chosen table. It was empty at that moment, which made it easier to make her mark. Joining in at a certain table probably wasn't important to anybody else, however, when it came to popularity, it was about putting a stamp on your social identity. All Maxine had to do was click on her charms and give it her all. It would have been nice for Gwen to join her for the occasion, but she'd decided to step back into the shadows, avoiding any exposure. Anyhow, Maxine was doing this for her own agenda. At least, her new gal pal Shawnie was corresponding.

"Are we allowed to sit here?" Shawnie asked worriedly.

"Sweetie, we have an obligation to sit here," Maxine purred nonchalantly. "Are we ugly by any chance?"

"Um...no."

"And are we wearing the best designer clothes?"

"...Yeah?"

Maxine curled a clever smile. "So we have nothing to worry about. Let's just sit back and let all the attention come to us."

Two of the girls arrived at the arranged table. There was Sondra, who was dazzling with her long wavy black hair and well-defined cheekbones, looking sexy and chic in a blue and green striped wool mini dress, her legs laced in designer stockings. And then there was Isabella, who was cute and petite, her hair full of strawberry curls and her eyes bright with apple green, dressed in a blue flowy top and denim jeans.

The two girls were not quite pleased at Maxine and Shawnie's intrusion.

"Um, excuse me, you're in our spot," Sondra said in a smug tone.

"Of course I am. I thought I would have a little welcoming for my arrival here. Maxine Triffendorf, nice to meet you." Maxine held out her hand, waiting for approval. The girls just stared at her, dumbfounded. Shawnie sunk into her chair, hoping the embarrassment of being shunned won't hurt her ego too bad.

"Perhaps we're getting off on the wrong foot," Maxine said, still turning on her sweet southern charm.

Sondra rolled her eyes and sat down at the table, eventually giving up. "Fine, we'll let you sit here. We just have to inform Bianca that we have some new acquaintances."

Maxine snorted, clearly forgetting her manners. "What is she, your boss or something?"

"No, we always sit here. It was our little spot since the beginning of school year," Isabella explained innocently.

"Oh." So it wasn't like someone had to be initiated to sit at a particular table. Maxine realized these girls were actually close friends, who had a sacred alliance, to which it was inconceivably disrespectful of her to barge in their territory. But she didn't care. Her focus was solely on making an impression.

"Since you're new here, tell us about yourself, uh, Maxine," Sondra said stiffly.

"Well..."

Maxine thought of a way to make a proper introduction. She wasn't going to tell them everything. She wasn't going to tell them about her transfer to North Carolina, the weight issues, and the money problems from before. Maxine had a way of talking without thinking; she could be her own worst enemy sometimes. What Maxine had to take was a shortcut. It wasn't a bad thing because in every instinct, a shortcut could get you very far in life.

She looked over at Shawnie, who'd been quiet throughout the whole conversation. She sat there, still and brittle, there were even beads of sweat forming on her forehead.

What is she so nervous about? Maxine thought. There were just sidekicks, the head honcho hadn't even arrived yet. Oh yes, Maxine was keeping an eye out for her.

She had to think of something quick.

"I was born in Atlanta, Georgia, great o'l peach state. My dad is the CEO of Bakersville Industries, and my mom usually hosts this annual fashion show where all these celebrities attend. The most famous attendees were Donatella Versace and Christian Siriano."

Sondra's and Isabella's faces lit up.

"My mom once did a photo shoot with Donatella Versace in the early two-thousands," Sondra beamed.

"Yeah, and my mom met Christian Siriano at one of his fashion shows," Isabella squeaked excitedly. "Oh, he makes the best shoes!"

Good. Maxine hooked them right in. Now for the facts: There was a yearly fashion show in Atlanta, but it wasn't hosted by Leigh-Ann; her great aunt Josephine was the hostess due to Maxine's cousin Analeigh being a successful fashion coordinator. Analeigh met with Donatella Versace at a Paris fashion gala, sending her an invitation to the Annual Atlanta Fashion Show. Analeigh also met Christian Siriano at an after-party in Los Angeles and then invited him to the annual fashion show a year later. Maxine only went to this event once for a family visit. Her cousin Analeigh had a way of blending in with the big leagues and Maxine might just use that exposure to help her in the end. It wasn't lying. It was simply twisting the facts to make it more accurate.

"I do like your outfit," Sondra complimented. "Fresh off the market?"

"Well, you can always get what money can buy, right?" Maxine said with her sly wink.

The two girls giggled lightly. Maxine had them where she wanted them. She was that good. She looked over at Shawnie again, seeing she'd mellowed a bit, seemed less intimidated. Now it was Sondra's and Isabella's turn to introduce themselves. Sondra was the sultry, cool one, the type of girl Maxine would definitely get along with. When the time came for Shawnie to open up, she meshed really well with Isabella, who was complimented by Shawnie's high-spirited optimism.

While the girls were heavy into conversation, Maxine could not help but glance at their almost empty lunch trays: A piece of romaine lettuce, low-fat dressing on the side, a cup of Jell-O, crackers, and broccoli.

How do these girls eat like this? Maxine thought. Since everybody was nice and comfortable, it was time to go in for the kill.

"Ladies, ladies, ladies. What am I seeing?" she said with concern.

"We're trying to be on a strict diet," Isabella explained.

Maxine scoffed dismissively. "Okay, that whole heroin chic look has been tossed out since the mid-nineties. Curvy is in. I mean, look at Shawnie, she has a nice body. Curvy but still fit."

The two girls bobbed their heads in agreement.

"It's okay to have a little tits and ass because that's what we're made of. So what if there are rules of fashion, fuck the rules. If the dress fits, it fits. It's as simple as that, girls."

"Hmm, very insightful," Sondra marveled.

A raven-haired girl came marching up to the table, clearly irked. She stopped her tracks, giving Maxine a sour look, as if eyeing an insect, waiting to be squashed. All Maxine could do was stare at her regal appearance, her stunning Ralph Lauren ensemble: a white satin top, a knee-length black skirt, and a black blazer. She looked so womanly. So professional.

"Who are you?" the girl demanded fiercely.

Maxine, with her coolest gesture, lazily stretched out her hand. "Maxine Triffendorf, at your service."

The girl just stared at Maxine and then turned her attention to Sondra and Isabella, not giving her the time of day. This must be the almighty Bianca. She knew she would get snubbed by her somehow. Maxine received all the information from Shawnie who was eager to ride up the popularity train. All she could talk about was Bianca and her posse. Piece. Of. Cake.

Maxine kept her sly smirk. Bianca's rudeness was a deflection, but her power was a reflection. All Maxine had to do was prick at her weak spot to break down whatever barrier her pride was kept in.

Bianca sat down at her table; a gloomy expression clouded over her face. Maxine kept her eye on her. *Not much for hiding emotions, eh?* Maxine deviously thought.

"Is there something wrong, Bianca?" Isabella asked in concern. "Where's Chace?"

Bianca propped herself up and haughtily straightened her blazer. "Chace doesn't sit here anymore."

"How come?" Sondra quizzed, curiously surprised.

"Because it's our table. Girls are much stronger than boys, so we have a right to our own table."

The other girls grew quiet, wondering whether they should ask the glaring question or leave it alone.

"Did something happen between you and Chace?"

Bianca took a deep breath to let it all sink in. She closed her eyes. "Chace and I...are no longer together."

Isabella covered her mouth, shocked from the revelation. "Gosh, B, that's terrible. What led to that decision?"

"He wants us to see other people," Bianca scoffed. "I just can't imagine myself doing that."

The unexpected bombshell grabbed Maxine's and Shawnie's curiosity. They sat silently observing every word.

"Listen, that is a perfectly natural thing. I mean come on, Bianca, you're only sixteen, there's plenty of boys to keep your eye on. I would think college boys would be more of your type. And now that you're newly single, Maxine is throwing this party on Friday," Sondra pointed out.

Bianca looked at Sondra blankly. "The only party I should be thinking about is the Kiss the Stars fundraiser," she said with barely concealed annoyance. "The fundraiser I told you about last week; you said you'd help out."

Maxine smirked. It was that easy. *Too bad, so sad.* She gave Shawnie a knowing sideways glance. It was all coming into formation.

Isabella blinked her eyes as if something hit her on the back of the head. "Oh. We, like, totally forgot..."

Bianca quickly collected her things and stood up firmly from the table. "You know, that's totally fine. I'll just go find somebody else to help with the party. Enjoy your little lunch with Maxine or whoever." Bianca stormed off, not even looking back.

"I feel so totally bad right now," Isabella winced.

"Girls," Maxine soothed. "Don't worry, she just had a really bad breakup. She'll be fine." Then Maxine had a devilish grin on her face. "By the way, can you tell me who this, uh, Chace is?"

The two girls giggled, obviously not that concerned he'd just dumped one of their closest friends. "Maybe if you join us at Bergdorf's this afternoon, we'll tell you about all the boys in Hamilton."

Maxine propped her hand on her chin. "That is a very generous offer."

The bell rang just as Maxine was starting to get comfortable.

"Well, ladies," Maxine said, standing in triumph. "We'll meet again."

Maxine sashayed down the hall while Shawnie gleefully tagged along.

"That went well, didn't it?" Shawnie perked, barely hiding her excitement.

"Oh yes, it certainly did."

The hick girl from the South was no more. It'll be a matter of time until she reached the Upper east side plateau.

Little Miss Bianca need to step aside...

There was a new girl in town.

◆   * *

NO SURPRISES

Gwen burst into the apartment and collapsed onto the couch, her body numbed with exhaustion. The day had been longer than she ever imagined a day could be. At school, everybody was watching her every move. Some even went out of their way to be up close to her. Like one of the freshman girls who ambushed her after lunch, asking for fashion tips as if she had any idea what name brand she was wearing, which was next to none. Then at third period, she could've sworn the guy sitting from behind her desk was touching strains of her hair. *How creepy.* Not to mention the suggestive stares of the junior and senior boys, aiming at her highly exposed legs. She didn't like it. She didn't like it at all. She'd always yearned for agency in her life, but this was way out of her league. It was too much pressure. Maybe it would be best if she stayed mute and wore gray for the rest of the school year, just so everybody would get off her back.

Out of any chance of being pursued by a boy, one in particular, had been unequivocally audacious. Chace Fairbanks had asked her out while still in a relationship with the school princess. If her life was a movie, she should press play now. It was as if the boy could get away with murder because of his good looks and sexy charm. How smarmy can a boy his age be? Guys like that repulsed her but they seem to be the norm at Hamilton Academy.

Gwen kicked off her pin-toed red heels and rolled over to the side, resting her head on the plush pillows. This was a time to get lost in her daydreams. She thought about the boy from the library, feeling his intense passion pouring through her body and soul. She visualized his honey-brown eyes. Tresses of dark curly red. Kissable lips. Mmm. Gwen drifted deep and further into her subconscious. She just couldn't get it out of her head, the thought of him was so livid. If there was a way she could see him again or find the confidence to speak if every ounce of her would

Then suddenly, the phone rang.

Gwen grabbed the receiver and sat up. "Hello?"

"Is this Gwen Stevenson?" The male voice on the line was high-pitched but serious in tone.

"Yes...This is she."

"Congratulations, Gwen! You're the winner of the fashion week giveaway contest!" the caller announced. "You will meet with fellow teen model Saleisha Roberts and receive free consumer products from our company..."

"Whoa, whoa, wait a minute. You must be mistaken. I didn't sign up for any contest," Gwen interrupted in disbelief.

"Your name is Gwen Stevenson, correct? I have your sample pictures in front of me right now."

Sample pictures? Gwen recalled back on that Saturday evening when she, Shawnie, and Maxine went shopping around Madison Avenue. Maxine asked Gwen if she could pose for a picture, just outside of the hair salon. Gwen had been reluctant, not feeling photo-ready with her new 'do. Furthermore, she was still dressed in her stained white T-shirt and faded jeans, not having the time to prep up such a task. Maxine, being Maxine, went ahead and took the pictures anyway. That girl sure did work fast.

"You know, sir, I will gladly accept the offer."

It was weird why they would choose her for the welcoming, though, she might as well enjoy it. Surely it could be something to write about in her diary. Because first of all, she wasn't really interested in this modeling thing, and after the whole meet and greet, the agency would probably lose interest anyway.

"Wonderful!" the man exclaimed cheerfully. "Be sure to come by the Madame Lasvar building in SoHo next Saturday afternoon. We'll have you pampered and prepped in no time. And trust me, many girls would die for this experience."

Yeah, die from their own misery, Gwen thought. She didn't really know what went on behind the closed doors of the modeling world, but from what Gwen read about, it was truly awful. Aside from that, the only thing concerning her was having a serious talk with Maxine...and finding some more comfortable shoes.

After receiving the strange phone call, Gwen quickly dialed Maxine's number.

"What the hell did you do?" Gwen demanded.

"What do you mean?"

"Don't play dumb with me, Maxine. I got a call from some fashion week contest."

"You won? That's great!" Maxine didn't bother being coy about it. "I can't believe you won! Yes!"

Gwen got the phone far from her ear until Maxine stopped her squealing.

"Now let me ask you again," Gwen said slowly. "What. The. Hell. Did. You. Do?"

"Don't get your panties in a bunch, girl, I'm only trying to better your position of certain opportunities. Do you know how much attention you'll get once the cameras are pointed at you? Oh, this is going to be great!"

"So tell me, Maxine, how did you come up with this ingenious plan?"

"Let's see," Maxine began playfully. "I was researching upcoming fashion week shows when I saw this ad on the Internet. All you needed was sample pictures, a distinctive, unique look, and references, which I so proudly inserted in myself. I was even able to charm the pants off the receptionist with all the stories I told her. They fall for it every time. The votes were in, and at the last minute, all my work was done."

"You just forged my name without consulting me?" Gwen said, flabbergasted.

"I thought it would be more suspenseful that way."

"I understand you're trying to help me, Max, but you're taking this too far."

"Gwen, darling...You'll thank me later. Oh, I can't wait to call Shawnie!" And just like that, Maxine hung up the phone.

"Maxine, wait..." But Gwen heard a distant click, and her friend was gone.

This was it. Feeling like the world was going to cave in on her for days on end.

Gwen couldn't decide which would be better: to be totally isolated or to have everybody watch your every move. Maybe isolation would be the best choice, just until things got a little more IN hand.

Gwen knew one thing from now on...

She sure as hell hated surprises.

J. D. Fitzgerald

SHE'S THE ONE

"Okay Roslyn, can you read over the line again?"

It was Monday afternoon at Central Park where Vera was on set to direct her new short film. She sat on her lawn chair, utterly disappointed at how the auditions turned out. Only four actresses lined up for the lead. There would've been eleven if there was any luck involved, but who was she kidding? She asked almost every girl in school to try out for auditions, but their response was what she expected: a little sugary ice to add to the venom.

"Sorry, gotta study for pop quiz, very important stuff," one girl said.

"Acting's not really my thing but thanks anyway," said another girl.

"I would rather work with a real director, no offense," said the last

girl.

There you have it, none to a fault without any convincing. Just as her options were beginning to run dry, she asked Roslyn Gruber if she could audition. Now, she hadn't expected her *Titan* co-editor to give a mind-blowing performance, but she had little effort or drive to embrace the role. Roslyn also complained about the lead character's motivation, being ever so critical of Vera's body of work. She was more on the business side of things, not at full level to step out of her comfort zone. Vera knew then it wouldn't work out. It wasn't so much the role or the feel of the movie, it was about an actor being "committed" to it. In between takes, Roslyn kept holding in fits and giggles every time she fumbled over the lines by covering her thick New York accent with a soft, British-like pitch.

What made the audition more embarrassing was that Roslyn was wearing a cheap blond wig, giving off a more comical effect. In the script, she envisioned Natasha as a waif-like blond. Roslyn had an indistinct shade of frizzy brown and a stocky frame. In desperation, Vera went racing to the costume store down the street to purchase a wig. It was no more than five dollars. The heat of the sun turned it into a strawed mess. The grueling procedure of bringing art to life was straining, leaving Vera no choice but to give Roslyn a pass.

"Okay Ross, you can go."

Roslyn ripped off the wig in victory. "Thank god, this thing was fucking itching me!"

Shawnie was her only hope.

To Vera's dismay, she immediately saw Shawnie wearing a saucy red dress, which was completely wrong for the type of role she was playing. Though the focus wasn't so much on the visual but more on the emotional aspect of the script.

"Shawnie, I hope you know what you're doing," Vera said worriedly.

"You can count on me, Ver," Shawnie replied cheerfully.

Shawnie recited her lines clearly and perfectly. Unfortunately, she didn't notice that while doing so, she had stuffed David's face under her bosom.

"Oh gosh, I'm so sorry," Shawnie panicked.

Vera sighed. "It's okay, Shawnie. Let's just do the scene again."

Shawnie obviously knew her lines but then suddenly kept blubbering over them, visibly nervous from the disastrous first take. Vera gave out a long-exasperated sigh. Shawnie was a sweet girl, but for her benefit, she needed experience.

And Vera wasn't looking for just any actress. She wanted a committed actress, somebody that would bring soul and essence to the character. Shawnie didn't seem to let go, feel natural. Turning away, as her eyes wandered off to the maple oak trees, Vera spotted a girl entering the park. The sun cast an illuminating glow over her hair, like a golden halo. She was dressed in a white short dress under a denim jacket, just how Vera envisioned Natasha, with expressive aqua eyes.

She's the one. She's the girl I've been looking for.

"Shawnie, I'll let you know about the casting details," Vera said dismissively.

She quickly approached the other girl, anxious to see her face-to-face. Her Natasha turned toward her.

"Gwen?" Vera said, surprised. "What are you doing here?"

"I just wanted to see how auditions was going."

Vera made a sly smile. "I had a few casting changes."

Gwen leaned against the tree. "How come?"

"Something suddenly came up," Vera said, her head slightly turning the other way. The words were falling out of her, she didn't know what to say. "How about you give it a try?"

Gwen was taken aback. It was odd that Vera would think she, with no little insight on acting, would have any potential to carry a film, let alone a short one. "I don't think I'm the right girl for you."

"Gwen, I can tell just by the look on your face, how passionate you really are. I must be an idiot to not have cast you before."

"You really think I could pull this off?" Gwen asked skeptically.

Vera wrapped her arm around Gwen's shoulders, leading her to the bench. "You have the look, and you definitely have the soul. I think this should go pretty well."

While following Vera to the other side, Gwen admired how beautiful Central Park was. She'd heard many stories and seen many pictures, though until recently, she'd never beheld it with her own eyes. It was like walking into a dreamland, with the trees changing in color and the sky painted light blue.

As Gwen reached toward the pond, she saw a mane of curly red hair resting on the bench. It was a boy who looked unkempt and shaggy in his baggy jeans and green plaid button-down. When he lifted his head and turned around, Gwen's eyes sparkled. So did his. She instantly remembered those honey-brown eyes of his, that beautiful curly hair, his milky white skin glimmering in the sunlight.

If she only knew his name.

"Okay, now that I can feel the chemistry already sizzling, let's skip the audition and begin filming," Vera said as she handed out the scripts. "Gwen, I'll give you some time to read out the scene before we shoot."

"Wait, Vera, I am so far from prepared."

"Don't worry, just go with the flow. I'll walk you through."

Sitting on the bench, Gwen read the rest of the script, but she stopped dead when she saw she had to kiss her co-star. Her stomach dropped. Was this really happening?

During this whole time, she hadn't said anything to the boy. Communication was a default, for when it came to boys, it wasn't Gwen's strongest point. Still, she had to remind herself, this was acting, not real life.

Three minutes later, shooting began.

Gwen froze on the bench, feeling the beating of her heart pounding like a hammer. She was actually going to kiss a boy on camera. This was so out of her element.

The boy slowly rested his head on her lap, staring at her with his enchanting brown eyes; Gwen was falling into a trance. Once Vera yelled, "Action," Gwen spoke the lines as if her whole heart was paved into them, as if every word she said was truth.

Then it was the moment. The kiss. Gwen leaned in, catching his breath. She felt a sense of warmth when their lips touched. An unfamiliar hot passion was growing inside her. She released the kiss, quivering from ecstasy.

"Cut," Vera said slowly, marveling at the scene that had happened in front of her. She rushed up to Gwen and shook her hand vigorously. "That was really good."

Gwen began shaking nervously, checking the time on her cell phone. "I'm totally late for something."

Just as she made a run for it, Vera caught up with her. "Gwen, what's the rush? That was fantastic."

Gwen was deeply overwhelmed. "Thanks, Vera. It's just...I'm kind of...tied up. I'll call you later, okay."

Gwen darted off to the woods but then she came to a halt. She gave one last glance at her co-star, their eyes met from afar. She waved him goodbye and continued.

That was the first time she'd ever truly felt something with a boy. A boy she hardly even knew. And yet, she was somehow scared of feeling this type of emotion that most girls yearned for. Time would tell if she kissed him again or at least got to know him first.

Because just by looking at him, she could feel his heat of passion as keenly as she felt her own.

◆   * *

PARTY AT THE PENTHOUSE

Everything was all set in Maxine's playbook. Friday night was the most important night to throw her first party in New York. Her parents, on a whim, decided to spend their weekend alone at Hampton beach and wouldn't be back until Monday morning. All Maxine had to do was pick up the phone, call Shawnie, Sondra, Isabella, the caterer, and...Presto! Her first Manhattan soiree was underway.

The party guests spread like wildfire. But the music wasn't too loud, and the alcoholic beverages were limited to wine and champagne instead of disgusting beer. Beer was by far the least favorite of her beverages and she didn't have any red solo cups for people to get stupid drunk on. This social event was going to be civilized.

Maxine sat on one of her French sofas and greeted Shawnie while sipping her white wine. "So how did your film audition go?"

Shawnie winced in embarrassment. "Not so good. So humiliating. I don't know if I'm as good of an actress as I think I am."

"Ah, don't worry about it. She's probably one of those artsy-fartsy directors with a stick up her ass. Just work on it. What comes after practice is perfection."

"Yeah, maybe I could do a Broadway show or two, If I'm lucky," Shawnie said dolefully, as she took a sip of her champagne. "I mean, Jayne Mansfield started out on Broadway."

"What you need is some cheering up," Maxine encouraged. "There are some very handsome senior boys that would love to meet you. Let's explore, shall we?"

Gwen and Kyle arrived, surprised to suddenly find themselves at a party. Maxine wanted to invite Gwen to "catch up on old times," possibly an apology for her rude behavior at lunch the other day. But as it turns out, it was one of Maxine's schemes biting her in the ass again. How quaint. Gwen's anxiety resurfaced, dressed in her unbecoming tie-dye T- shirt and ripped jeans.

Maxine walked up to them with her hand on her hip and a sly smile on her face. "Gwen, you're not properly dressed." She took Gwen's hand and pulled her towards the bedroom. "Come on, I got some clothes for you to try on."

Kyle swiftly blocked Maxine from the pathway, her arms firmly crossed. "What the hell is going on here? You didn't tell us about a party."

"Oh yeah, a few other friends stopped by." Maxine chuckled. "Greet, socialize, knock yourself out." She gazed at Kylie's green pantsuit. "Oh and, love the outfit." After that, Maxine briskly carried Gwen off to the bedroom.

Entering the room, Gwen sprawled across the bed, staring at the ceiling. "Why do you do this?"

Maxine rummaged through her closet absentmindedly. "What?"

"Put me in these situations?"

Maxine stopped and looked at Gwen thoughtfully, trying to think of something profound to say. She slowly sat beside Gwen, her arms around her shoulder. Maxine gave her a comforting smile, feeling protective of her friend. "Gwen, I just want us to embrace life and not feel sorry for ourselves. Being liked, being loved, being a part of something. I want to be able to spend those moments with you."

Gwen can see the urgency in Maxine's expression. She really was genuine and still seems to have that spark, that desire to be accepted. "That's very sweet, Max. But why some part of me thinks this is some personal quest of yours."

"Okay, let's get real here. From what I can see, these girls are much worse than Amber Krecther, So I can use some backup. It's the ultimate bitch you have to watch out for. But like they always say, if you can't beat 'em, join 'em."

"Why does it have to be that way?" Gwen said, harboring a sick feeling. "It's such bullshit."

Maxine tenderly patted down Gwen's hair. "We're not in North Carolina anymore, honey. And at this point in our lives we have to be prepared. Because in New York, it's a dog- eat-dog world. I'm only trying to look out for you, Gwennie."

Gwen felt that fiery determination Maxine had since she was ten years old, something she always admired. It wouldn't be so bad when she thought about it. It was a party just like any other party. You socialize, you greet, you get it over with. This was her chance to finally break out and see what this new lifestyle would bring. It took baby steps, tiny little baby steps to come out of her shell.

Gwen smiled. "Fine. What the hell."

"Great," Maxine squeaked, springing up excitedly. "Now, let's get you fixed up. There's a special somebody waiting for you outside."

Gwen raised an eyebrow. "Who might that be?"

Maxine mischievously pressed her finger to her lips. "Shh, it's a surprise."

Dressed in a low-cut black dress too tight around her waist and stiletto heels torturing her arches, Gwen followed Maxine to see a group of four boys standing in a huddle. Her stomach turned. Too bad the tight dress didn't help. Then, with a shocking sureness, Gwen knew what special surprise Maxine had in store for her...

Chace Fairbanks.

And his jock buddies, no less. How typical of Maxine. What kind of fantasy world did she live in? What made her think that this guy, who had an impossible reputation, could be the perfect catch. And not to mention, his darling girlfriend was under her radar. Nope, He was definitely NOT the one.

"Ah, you must be Chace," Maxine greeted smoothly, casting him flirty eyes. "I would like you to meet a friend of mine, Gwyneth."

Gwen faced him, staring into those familiar midnight blues, not so fooled by them anymore. He might be a jerk, but it was certainly hard to look away from his stylish tuxedo, which made his eyes even bluer.

Maxine swished her hips as she glided over to a spiky-haired boy. "And you must be Austin."

The boy took Maxine's hand, kissing it gently. "Pleasure."

"Why don't you two go talk in the study," Maxine said with an indiscreet wink at Gwen. "Austin and I would like to get to know each other."

While Maxine and her companion went away to their own devices, Gwen stood stock-still, not stepping one foot close to Chace. His reaction to her quiet reception was a shy smile. A shy, boyish smile, which melted her just a bit. It wasn't an act. Gwen stood her stance and kept her expression cold.

"Would you like to go to the study, so we can talk? The music is kind of loud," Chace said politely. He put his hand to her waist, but she flinched and crossed her arms. Gwen didn't say anything. She didn't want to look at him. Some part of her did like Chace, but she just didn't want to be a fool for his charms. And she certainly didn't want to be his "other woman."

There were so many girls who felt humiliated or stupid after going on that one special date with the boy of their dreams. Only to have their hearts crushed, as a ploy of some cruel, vindictive prank. Gwen wanted no part of this preppy rich-kid drama. Would Chace be any different? She didn't think so. But she had to trust her instincts. Let the hunter to be hunted.

In the study, Gwen sat in the plush love seat, gazing into the dancing fire. She still didn't say a word. Although it wasn't because she was being standoffish but diffident. Being alone in a room with a guy made her so nervous, she felt paralyzed in the chair. Chace sat beside her, about an inch away. She refused to look back at him.

"Is something the matter? We don't seem to be talking much," Chace said, with a simple chuckle.

Gwen suddenly felt her skin warm and finally looked at him but kept her restraint. "Why should we?"

Chace was clueless. "What do you mean?"

Gwen rolled her eyes. "Don't you have a girlfriend?"

Chace winced as he turned his head away, but then faced her. "I...I broke up with her recently."

"How convenient," Gwen retorted. "I wonder why that happened."

"We were just in different circumstances."

"And so you thought you could come to *me* all of a sudden? Is it because I'm pretty now?"

"It's not like that. I've liked you from the first day I saw you."

Gwen stood up and glanced at the John Waterhouse painting over the fireplace. It was titled *La belle dam sans mercie*, depicting a young maiden seducing a knight with her long flowy hair. Was this telling her something?

"This brings up the question of WHY do you like me. You don't even know me."

Chace pondered, scratching his head. "But I'd like to. Let's get to know each other. Start off fresh."

Gwen looked at him quizzically. "You really think that's possible?"

"Yeah, I do. I'll tell you something about me, and then you tell me something about yourself. But first, let's get the hell out of here before somebody starts thinking the inevitable."

"Oh yes, let's get out of here before the hyenas catch us," Gwen said sarcastically, however, She had a slight grin on her face and that familiar twinkle in her eye.

She still had an emotional barrier but felt a little more comfortable by using her dry sense of humor as a weapon. Whatever he had up his sleeve, she had enough wit to cut him down a peg.

Chace slowly opened the door for her. "After you."

Gwen's cheeks blushed a bright red glow. When was the last time a guy opened the door for her?

Central Park was even more beautiful at night. The moon glowed over the rosebushes and lily beds, making them look like flower lamps. The bright green grass glistened like a shimmering emerald sea. The Autumn leaves rustling within the trees, changing from green to gold. Gwen could not believe summer was almost over; the night was beautiful this time of year.

Walking along the pond creek, Chace begin to narrate his home life. Gwen was astonished by how incredibly ordinary and humble he was. He described his father as a Gordon Gekko type with a bit of a controlling streak, always putting on the pressure for Chace to become the next cooperate leader of the Wall Street industry. His mom, Delilah, was a

French heiress who owned an event planning company and traveled extensively around Europe, serving her globe-trotting clients. From Chace's point of view, Delilah took her job way too seriously. She expected everything to be perfect, all the time, especially at parties and dinner arrangements. It made Gwen uncomfortable when he compared her to Bianca, a perfectionist herself. But maybe he was trying to tell her why he broke up with her: he didn't want to date someone like his mother.

Throughout all this...Chace tried to live his life as normally as he could. Playing Xbox with his friends, hanging out at burger joints, watching sports, etc. It was like talking to a regular guy.

Once the two of them sat on the bench, Gwen began telling her story but not getting as deep into it as Chace had. Gwen told him about her life and times in North Carolina and confided how scary it was to move to a new city where she seemed to be on everybody's radar. For better...or worse.

"Back in the summer before seventh grade, I found this stray puppy I kept as a pet. The first time that little dog laid eyes on me, I knew we were going to be inseparable. I named him Pepper because he had chestnut brown fur with black spots." Gwen looked at the sky serenely, thinking of that memory. "Me, Mona, and Maxine would spend afternoons in the backyard, playing with him for hours. Pepper was so full of energy. Like this jovial soul of life...But then at the end of summer..." Gwen's face darkened. "Pepper got hit by a van. I was just a block away and chased after him when it happened. He'd been spooked by some idiot shooting off fireworks and ran off."

"You must have been devastated," Chace sympathized.

"Yeah, I was. But do you know what's strange? It was like some metaphor of how to let go of things when your life is just beginning." Although the story was true, that wasn't the story Gwen had intended to tell. It was the first few days of summer without her father. All she had was written letters, making promises he couldn't keep. She tried to block that devastating pain of loss...Not from a pet or even a friend...but...from a parent.

"I used to have this pet mouse name Jeffery when I was six." Chace took Gwen's hand, she hesitated but feeling the warmth of his touch, she relaxed. "I kept him in this little shoe-box while I was at school. Then one day, one of the maids found him...and when I got home, I found the smashed shoe-box on the sidewalk. I opened it up and all I could see was blood, Jeffery's mutilated body smashed in the middle. Pretty horrific sight for a first grader."

Gwen winced. "God, how awful."

"Definitely was. Some people think it's odd being so emotionally attached to pets, but when you're a kid, it's something special."

Gwen looked up at the moon, so full and bright, though there were few stars out. The city was clouded with light pollution, cleared out into a purple lining in the sky. One of things she missed from her home state was how the stars twinkled like diamonds, high above the mountains. Back in those innocent days of early childhood, she would hop on her dad's shoulders, reaching out to catch a falling star. But the night was crisp and full of marvel, seeing the glittery waves of the pond creek, reflecting the moonlight. And here she was sitting next to a guy with eyes the color of the midnight sky. Then those familiar feelings started to come up again. The same feelings she had when she'd first laid eyes on him.

"Do you ever stargaze?" Gwen asked softly.

"Not much, no."

"It matches the color of your eyes." She hoped that didn't sound corny. She didn't know if it was her impulses or her hormones, but the words sort of came out somehow.

Chace smoothed Gwen's hair. "You know, when I look in your eyes, it reminds me of the times I would stare out at the clear blue skies in the Hamptons. Such beautiful, beautiful days."

From that moment, the two of them gazed into each other. Those feelings started up again and then they finally took over. He pulled her into his kiss, letting him sink into her instantly, yet it was different from her co-star's kiss. Yes, *the co-star.* She hadn't even thought about him. Then Gwen realized that right here on this very spot was the same spot she'd kissed the boy. She pulled back, feeling a strange twinge of guilt.

"It's...It's getting kind of late," Gwen said in a nervous whisper.

"Do you want me to take you home?"

Gwen wanted to run away but knew running alone through Central Park at night was a stupid move. She reluctantly decided to go with him instead. "Sure."

She felt special to be with Chace Fairbanks, Hamilton Academy's prize catch. But at the same time, she felt terrible, as dark as the dress Maxine picked out for her. The temptress caught in the middle of two desirable suitors. She didn't want to be that type of girl, yet this was something she had always hoped for: to share a kiss with the boy of her dreams.

But deep in her mind, she begin to wonder...Where will her heart lead to?

Maxine giggled girlishly at Austin's dirty jokes, admiring his skin-tanned glow. He was a diamond in the rough. This tough Bronx guy hidden underneath a funny and charming disposition. He wasn't as tall as she'd expected him to be, but at least he was tall enough to kiss face-to-face. **IF** that ever happened. And at least he wasn't like those annoying guidos she'd seen on TV, even though he unfortunately sounded like one, but nobody's perfect. She tried to subdue her embarrassingly loud country cackle that seemed to belt out unpredictably. Again, nobody's perfect. So she forced herself to laugh in an eloquent yet cutesy way in public. Especially when there was a guy around her. She knew she was playing it just right: interested, entertained, but not easy. To top it all off, she wore her alluring Dior purple mermaid dress, to which Austin can't keep his eyes off of.

Over at the bar, Shawnie was having a grand o'l time with Blake Kingston. Maxine didn't approve. Given that Shawnie was a hopeless romantic, Maxine tried to set her up with Kenny. Maybe a sensitive artist could sweep off her feet. But in between the last two senior boys, Kenny and Jeremy, Blake Kingston, decked out in a tuxedo straight out of an 80's music video, caught Shawnie's eye. When Maxine first met him, he had this cocky sense of arrogance she can't seem to pass over. He had a stunning resemblance to Tom Cruise, but his looks were too cookie-cutter for her taste. He had no edge to him, he was just *bland*. He so smoothly introduced himself as 'future heir of Lockhart and Galveston', hoping to become the poster boy of New York City advertising. His smarmy approach didn't faze Maxine, but Shawnie was openly flattered.

Yuppie boy on a WASPy platter, Maxine thought. *You sure picked a good one, Shawnie.*

He had quite the wondering eye as well, glancing at each passing girl when Shawnie wasn't noticing. She was just so mesmerized by Blake's charms, she couldn't consider anyone else. There was nothing left to do but just let her dive deep into aesthetic bliss.

When Austin went to fetch her another glass of white wine, Maxine waltzed over to Kyle, who was chatting with Jeremy Fletcher. From the look of things, Kyle wasn't at all impressed by Jeremy. Although there was a mutual attraction on Jeremy's part, nothing was really hitting off, the chemistry was a dud. Maxine's logic of opposites attract was irrelevant. Kyle, the intellectual, and Jeremy, the athlete, were a mismatched pair for sure.

Maxine slid beside Kyle and gave her a sly look as Jeremy excused himself to leave the girls alone. "What do you think of hot stuff over there?"

"Definitely not my type," Kyle scoffed.

"Why not? He's tall, handsome, and athletic."

"Those are only the physical qualities of him. Personality wise, not so much. I can't even have an intelligent conversation with him."

"Kyle, you're a smart girl. Some guys just can't catch up with that. But don't worry, Jeremy's not the only boy who has his eye on you," Maxine said as she winked.

"Oh please, do you really think..." Kyle paused for a moment. "Wait a minute...Why am I talking to you about this? Why am I even still here?"

"Listen, sweetie, live for the moment and get yourself a cocktail." As Maxine strolled away, she stopped and looked over her shoulder. "Cause you sure as hell deserve it." With that, Maxine strutted to the living room.

She found Shawnie, resting on the chaise lounge, as if she was floating in a blissful dream. The girl was trapped, not only in her lack of judgment, but in a world farthest from reality. Maxine can see that Blake Kingston wasn't all that special, but on top of that, Shawnie was a wee bit tipsy, letting her inhibitions slide.

"How's lover boy?" Maxine asked, sarcastically.

"He's the perfect gentleman," Shawnie gushed.

"Shawnie, I just don't know about him. I could've sworn I've seen him grope half the girls when you weren't looking."

"Oh, he's probably fooling around like most boys do," Shawnie replied nonchalantly. "If

you say so. But whether or not, he's fucking those girls, I can't answer that for you."

"Oh Maxine, you're so silly," Shawnie tittered.

"Have you drunk all the wine?"

Then standing there with a smug sureness on his face, Blake bowed his head in a gentlemanly fashion. "I hope I haven't interrupted your conversation, ladies."

"Oh you're no trouble at all, my dear sir," Maxine said in a mocking tone, rolling her eyes.

Maxine let out a sigh of relief as Austin came by with a glass of wine. She daintily received the crystal wineglass, giving Austin her best million-dollar smile.

"I guessed sparkling wine is your favorite," Austin said suavely.

"It certainly is, Romeo," Maxine parried smoothly.

Blake gently held Shawnie's hand as she hovered close to him, like an invisible elastic band was attached to them. "We'll leave you two alone, you must be very busy," Blake said, nuzzling Shawnie's neck, making her constantly giggle.

Maxine kept her eyes on Austin. "Please, make yourselves at home."

Shawnie wrapped her arms around Blake's neck, smelling his Calvin Klein cologne as she followed him up the stairs to the guest room. *Blake.* Saying his name, she felt a warm sensation in her body. It was like some hormonal drive she couldn't control. Here she was. Having just met this guy, and already she was falling deep. She suspected her mom would call it boy crazy.

But Shawnie knew her attraction to Blake was more than that. He had those debonair and chivalrous ways about him, emulating a fifties movie star. He was so suave, in fact, Shawnie really didn't stop to think where all this was heading. It was this moment. Right here, right now. Lying on the bed in Blake's arms. Wait, what was she doing on the bed? Maybe she had a little too much to drink, which would explain the strange sensation she was having.

"Blake, I have a question," Shawnie asked, while resting her head on his chest. "How, do you know me?"

"I had my eye on you for quite a while," Blake said without blinking an eye. "But I guess Ian old boy beat me to it."

Shawnie laid back against the pillows, almost laughing at the memory of Ian. "Oh please, we weren't even that serious."

There was a relationship there, but it wasn't meant to be. Shawnie was so lost in the moment, the thought of Ian was completely wiped from her mind. She looked deep into Blake's vale green eyes with sudden certainty.

"I'm getting lost into you," she said in a breathy sigh. She could feel the full moon was doing something to her, letting herself disappear into the clouds.

Blake caressed her hand. "Well I'm yours for the takin'."

She fell into his kiss, surrendering to her sudden passion. It was just like those summer nights on the beach, back in the Malibu shores. Feeling the touch, the warmth, the smell of a man she yearned for.

The night was young. And so were they.

J. D. Fitzgerald

LIVING POETS SOCIETY

David sat at his desk, desperately in need to commence the words of his next poem. There were so many words to describe the girl who'd touched his lips so softly yet passionately; he could remember it so vividly. How the sun kissed her hair, how her eyes glowed beneath the ray of light, shining behind her as she bent her lips to his. There were so many other girls he could've shared that moment with; he'd been at Vera's mercy. But this girl. This particular girl did something to him. She made him whole.

The journey to Hamilton started back at the fall of freshman year. However, it was an opportunity he didn't quite expect. His first poem had been "The Red-Haired Lady." Though the outlet of the piece was very personal to him, not really to be shared by anyone.

He opened the cupboard right above the desk and took a glance at the photo of his parents. It was a portrait of a couple, young, wild and free, ready to explore the world. Evidently, the reality of life was what tore them apart.

After inheriting the east Brooklyn sports bar, owned by his late uncle Sam, Ronald was finishing up his college terms while brainstorming the family business with the help of Sam's longtime business partner and financial adviser Bill Howitzer. Ronald first met Laura while she worked as a waitress there, having just moved in with relatives after a brief stint at Wisconsin State College. From how Ronald would describe her, as he told David, Laura had this immensely alluring charm, accumulating a personality that was both sexy and funny. And after three weeks of just knowing each other, it was a whirlwind courtship. Ronald proposed to Laura once the business started picking up, having their summer nuptials at the Grace Hill chapel church. By the time David was born in late fall, Laura decided to quit her job at the sports bar to become a full-time parent. But as she was known to be a fun-loving thrill seeker, the duties of being a sheltered housewife was putting a continuous amount of strain on Laura. She decided to get a receptionist job at a trading business company, in which she spent working late as a cover up for her frequent bar-hopping with her co-workers. As little as David can remember, his parents barely fought. When Ronald confronted about her late nights at work, Laura would respond in a careless reply, mentioning "extra work assignments." Simple as that. No communication. No discussion. He just accepted it. And therefore, it was the beginning of the end.

David rested his head on his hand, closing his eyes. The memories were triggering him. He had only been five years old, anxious to see his mother coming home. Peeking out the window, he saw something that truly perplexed him. His mom was kissing a man who didn't look like his father. That memory haunted him, planting the seeds of what was to come.

It was a month later on a typical Saturday afternoon. David could remember sitting in the living room, noticing the two suitcases by the door. His mom was wrapped in a trench coat, her red hair long past her shoulders, looking beautiful as ever. She held a stoned expression on her face but once she looked at David, fresh tears begin to roll down her cheeks. She covered her mouth, choking in sobs, as she knelled before him. David patted the top of his mother's head as his way of consoling her, although he didn't know what was going on. She looked up with a sad smile, kissing his hand, his forehead and whispered a soft, somber "I love you," to his ear.

Turning away, she grabbed the suitcases and went out the door. That was the last he would ever see of her. From then on, David always had a romanticized view of his mother, hearing the stories his father used to tell about her, though still not fully realizing her betrayal. But as he got older, he felt that pain and anguish. At the age of eleven, he put those feelings into words. He spent hours every day after school in his room, studying poetry and writing in his notebook. Worrying about his son's lack of socializing, Ronald persuaded David to join the boy scouts during the summer. He was amused at his dad's suggestion. However, as a blessing to his father, he insisted.

To David's surprise, he met a friend. His name was Zeke, a heavy-set kind of kid, who had an immense love of comic books and horror films. David eventually joined him at Edward B Shallow Middle School, taking a small break from writing until the end of seventh grade.

During that summer, he took more time to look back on his old poems. One such poem sparked an interest in him, the first one he wrote since he was eight. He reconstructed it, gave it a flow, and gave it a new title. Then eighth grade came by. David was strolling around the halls before first period, when he spotted out an ad on the bulletin board. It was for a poetry contest held at the Powerhouse arena. David was enlightened, but he was very reluctant to show his poem at first. He wasn't sure if he was ready to face the millions of crowds or for anybody to criticize his work, though, there was something in the back of his mind that persuaded him to take the leap. And out of the blue, he got in. Then he went to the citywide competition, earning the scholarship to Hamilton Academy. A school he wasn't sure he belonged to but was too good of an academic opportunity to miss.

For his first day, he wore his favorite *Regular Show* t-shirt, tamped down his curly hair, and put on his dad's worn-out loafers. These were the awkward years, still having freckles on his face, still a little clumsy, and still having to go through puberty with his tall, lanky figure. The kids found him odd and off-putting, amused by his gawky appearance. Most of the Hamilton pupils seemed to sail effortlessly through puberty, unlike David. He decided to go incognito, taking the role of high school outcast. He'd written a good poem, and this was where it brought him. A school full of people who didn't acknowledge or even care if he was there.

But someone did eventually care and that someone was Vera. It started off weird. She had a semi-crush on him, which he didn't understand because he wasn't like a stud or anything. Then a weirdly unemotional kiss had brought them together during those tribal times, and they developed a closer platonic relationship. Vera was the only one who gave him confidence, overcoming his self-effacing demeanor at Hamilton.

So, it wasn't like he was a total loser. It wasn't like he was alienated from the rest of existence. Therefore, this was his final year in high school and still he had no girlfriend. As it may, the girl from Central Park lake might be the one for him. If only he could know her name. *Gwen.*

Gwen, like Lady Gwen of air, blowing in the autumn winds...

Reminiscing about that image in the park put a spark in his mind and he instantly begin to write.

Her hair gleaming in the ray of sunshine, her eyes enchanting, and her lips full and moist...

Every word felt real, born of the passion he felt for her.

Lady Gwen of air, her hair bloomed and blossomed like the flowers in the mist.

He knew he would see her again. And one day, he'd have his chance.

◆ * *

GUESS WHO'S COMING TO DINNER

Gwen woke slowly from her slumber, drifting in and out between sleeping and waking. She finally forced her eyes open, staring at the ceiling. She thought about last night when she'd kissed Chace. Gwen felt frigid on the cab ride home, sitting just inches away from him in the backseat. The kiss should've broken the ice by now, but it made Gwen freeze up her emotional wall even more. So she didn't exactly wrap up the evening with a nicely knit bow. She was stagnant, bringing the air of awkward silence during the whole ten minutes. As the cab stopped at her apartment, Gwen looked at Chace, contemplating how she would end the evening. A hug? No, too intimate. A kiss on the cheek? Fuck no, mixed signals. She decided on a firm handshake.

"Thank you for a lovely evening," she said in skittish chirp.

There it was, starting off great but ending on a dud. Though, as Gwen begin to wonder, where did the guilt come from? She kissed two guys in a row, was that such a crime? The first kiss was for a movie scene while the second happened out of…As she would call it, a spur-of-the-moment type of thing. Big deal. If anything, Gwen should be proud of herself. She never thought a girl of such social inadequacy could ever accomplish that feat.

Gwen turned over, diving deep under the covers. Maybe if she slept a little longer, she could forget how embarrassing last night was…

While buried under the pillow, Gwen smelled a strong perfume scent only her mother could wear. She turned her head around, holding her sneeze.

"Mom?" Gwen groaned, annoyed. "What is it?"

"Hey, sweetie," Susan said singsong voice. "Guess what?"

Gwen sunk back into her pillow. "What?"

"I've just been invited to a lunch party!" Susan beamed in a perky tone.

"How did you get the invite?"

"You know that story I was working on about the workers' strike at the Bernstein company? Well, yesterday, out of the blue, Neal Walworth, who owns this big-deal law firm, called and thanked me for making the story public. And now that he's representing the workers in the civil case trial, he invited *me* to his celebration party. Which starts today at…"Susan checked her watch. "…two-clock. So whadda say, baby girl, ready to hit the town?"

Gwen popped up from the bed. "Today? And what part do I have in this exactly?"

"It's a good thing Neal has a daughter your age. Okay, the gist is, you keep her entertained while I get the details on the trail. Don't worry, I've already got the perfect dress for you to wear."

"Mom, is it really that important? I don't feel like being around a bunch of rich snobs today," Gwen mumbled in disdain.

"Of course, sweet pea. This company embezzled *millions* from other countries, wavered *down* their employee's income, I have to get all of the nasty details. Now are with me on this?" Susan said, her eyes widened in expectation. "I do need some support."

Gwen sighed. She had to give it to her mom, she was a master at persuasion. "Fine, fine, I'll go. At least there will be something to do on the weekend, I guess."

"That's my girl. We have to be prepared by exactly one-thirty. Be sure to keep an eye on that clock."

As Susan left the room, Gwen rested her head back on the pillow. Gwen begin to ponder a little. Walworth. That last name sounded familiar. There was only one person she could think of with that name. He also had a daughter… Then it hit her. Bianca Walworth. She was going to *her* dad's celebration party. How was this even possible? To go to a personal luncheon with a girl who probably hated her guts? This day was not going to end well. Misery was heading near.

Gwen felt a chill down her spine. She looked up at the tall brick townhouse. She was going *inside* Bianca's house. She slowly climbed up the concrete steps, her heart pounding with each thud. When she arrived, Gwen marveled at the interior décor of the living room, leading off to the dining room. It had an antique flair of the Victorian age, with its gold diamond shapes on the marble floor and the creamy white wallpaper, blending in well with the dark red velvet furniture. Gwen couldn't believe her eyes, it was something out of a Home and Garden magazine.

The guests were spread out, making their way to the dining room. To keep away from eye contact, Gwen read out the invitation list, scanning out each individual last name. The Parkases and their daughters, Sondra and Sonja. The Comptons and their daughter Isabella and son Marcus. The Kingstons and their sons Blake and Sal. And the Fairbankses and their son Chace...oh no.

Chace Fairbanks was here at the party as well.

Gwen was sinking deeper and deeper into the rabbit hole. How can this get any *worse?* So it made sense why Bianca and her crew had such a tight knit around each other, making her relationship with Chace that much more special. Gwen thought she was so crappy for putting herself into this predicament. From the moment Gwen entered the dining room, she spotted out the sitting arrangements. The Parkases were at the right side of the first row, the Comptons at the right of the second row, the Kingstons far end at the left, the Fairbankses was placed beside the Walworths, who sat at the center of table.

Being the guest of the hour, Gwen was required to sit in front of the almighty Bianca, who stared at her like a hawk in her Dior black evening dress. Chace was glancing at Gwen from afar, which put a dour expression on Bianca's face.

"So, Susan, I heard you've done some humanitarian work," Neal Walworth said amiably.

Susan perked up, always eager to chat about her charity causes. "Yes, I have. I volunteered helping the Hurricane Katrina victims, I raised money for breast cancer, I volunteered as a drug counselor, and I protested for workers' aid."

"Impressive," Neal replied with a jolly chuckle. "My wife and I have hosted a few charity events."

Bianca rolled her eyes.

"How interesting that our daughters go to the same school," Marla Walworth noted politely.

"Oh yes, my Gwen is having a wonderful time at Hamilton," Susan gushed.

Gwen made a sour face, examining the elaborate cuisine before her: caviar hors d'oeuvres followed by finely cooked filet mignon and creamed spinach. Had she ever tasted something like this in North Carolina? And whatever her mom said about enjoying Hamilton was bogus. Sure, it didn't turn out as bad as Gwen thought, but there was always an avalanche of drama along the way, spreading from one source to another. This was high school after all.

"Gwen and Bianca must have lots to talk about." Marla planted a hand on Bianca's shoulder. "Isn't that right, dear?"

Bianca narrowed her eyes at Gwen. "Yes. I have plenty," she agreed in a surgery yet menacing tone while downing a whole glass of red wine in one gulp.

Gwen's anxiety was kicking in her bloodstream. She couldn't stand it any longer. All she could do was wish this day was over, wish she could escape the trappings of this never-ending soap opera that was beginning to be her life.

Bianca sat on her tufted Victorian sofa, observing the party guests. She can hear Sondra and Isabella cackling at Blake's crude sex jokes as they strolled with him side by side, invading Bianca's space.

"Care to join us, Bianca?" Sondra asked.

She detected the sugary, fake tone in Sondra's voice, indicating that their casual conversation was about her.

She hastily stood up, smoothing out the lines of her black dress. "No thanks. I'll just be on my own."

The gossip was spreading quickly. The topic of Chace and his wandering eye was seeping at bay. What she so desperately wanted to do was spend time alone to collect herself, but the only hideout she could think of was the study, her former childhood playroom.

Bianca entered the study and sat in the large green armchair. She rested her head in her hands, trying to cry out whatever she was holding inside. But she couldn't. She just couldn't. All there was left to do was simply ponder what was boggling her mind.

Sondra and Isabella must've had a field day laughing at her expense, whispering the most ridiculous stuff they could come up with. Not only did they gossip with each other, they gossiped with Blake, who had the biggest mouth of them all. Why the hell was she ever friends with these people? To think of it, her life was sealed the day she was born.

Neal Walworth and Peter Fairbanks were old college buddies in Harvard, networking from colleague to colleague. They had a sort of complex friendship, having their professional differences before a fair comprise. Her father would tell humorous stories to his circle of friends of how if he and Peter made a bet, upon when the day Bianca and Chace get married, they'd cosign on a business merger.

Fat chance of that ever happening, Bianca thought bitterly.

Her parents were like machines, pushing for money and power to fuel their satisfaction. It was about keeping up appearances, trying your best, and reaching the status quo. Bianca reluctantly had to follow their legacy. Still, at that moment, she proceeded to strive for a higher purpose. To wear the best clothes, to be beautiful, to be smart, to be successful. Those were the key ingredients to life. Especially in a place like New York. But the decline of her only romantic relationship and the loss of respect she had from her peers gave Bianca an epiphany. It was time for a change, to see things from a different perspective. From the week before, she thought about switching schools, sailing off from the confines of Hamilton. She'll make sure the Kiss the Stars party would be her last hurrah before her grand exit. Did she think anybody should care? Not likely.

Suddenly, she heard someone enter the room. She peeked out from behind the chair. Bianca recognized the shimmer of blond hair...

Well, what do you know, speak of the devil, Bianca thought.

Dressed up in a peach-colored cocktail dress perfect for a debutante, she was everything but the equivalent of Sandra Dee. Her mannerisms were milquetoast, learning her p's and q's, saying yes ma'am and no sir at the table. She saw how this girl was completely out of her element. However, Bianca saw the look of distress reflected in the brass oval mirror. The concept of empathy was uncommon to her, though she shouldn't judge this girl.

When she heard about her arrival from North Carolina, Bianca assumed that the girl was a trailer trash reject, who'd struck it rich with that grand o'l opportunity to come to a place like New York. But...she wasn't. Right now, she was some ingénue lost in a world full of people she didn't understand.

All day at the table, Gwen had seemed humble, quiet, and not at all excited about Chace's attention. And her mom seemed like a cool person, too, doing what she could for other people, far more than her own family would do. Bianca felt too tired to declare war on this girl, but she honestly wasn't sure how else to play it safe and keep her reputation intact. Then she had a radical idea. Bianca held her breath and stood up from the chair, clearly startling the other girl.

"I...I'm sorry, I was just looking for the bathroom," the girl stammered. "I got lost along the way. I didn't mean to intrude."

"It's fine," Bianca responded calmly. "Most people would get lost in a place like this."

There was a long moment of silence until Gwen hesitantly turned for the door.

"No, wait." Bianca found the courage to go through her plan. "Look, I know you have a thing for Chace," she said firmly but not accusatory.

"Bianca, it's not like that, I swear..."

"But what girl wouldn't?"

"Bianca, I couldn't do that to you." Gwen looked at the floor in guilt.

"Don't feel bad," Bianca reassured. "It's actually been over between us for a while; it's just that we hadn't realized it. But let me tell you one thing...A boy like Chace Fairbanks, has a lot of baggage."

Bianca met Gwen's eyes; a look of sadness cast over her cat-violets. Not sharp nor severe but vulnerable. Then Bianca smiled sadly, leaving the room in quiet desolation.

Gwen was paralyzed with shock. *What just happened?* Did Bianca just offer her to Chace? That wasn't the Bianca she knew so far. The girl standing before her was a girl coming to terms with losing a boy she loved for so long, which made it hard for Gwen to accept such a fate. Then there was the question of emotional baggage. What did Chace do to her to make her say that?

Susan interrupted her reverie by poking her head through the study door. "Oh, there you are. Come on, hon, I'm ready to go."

"I'll catch up with you, Mom."

"I'll go hail a cab; meet me out in the front."

Gwen walked into the hallway, still getting lost in her thoughts. Her mind in deep concentration, she bumped full face into Chace, staring at his divine features. Chiseled cheeks, cupid bow lips, those alluring midnight blues of his. He was deliciously irresistible.

"Hey," Chace greeted with a smirk.

"Hey," Gwen replied bashfully.

"I want to make up for last night, I didn't mean to freak you out...but I was wondering...if you like to go out on a date?"

"Chace, I don't want things to be complicated as it is."

Chace held Gwen's hands. "Trust me, I'll be the perfect gentleman."

Gwen was a bit reluctant as she thought about what Bianca told her. But still...It wouldn't hurt, right? Just one date, just to see how it turned out.

"Um," Gwen hesitated. "Okay. Sure."

"Great! I'll pick you up on Friday. What's your number?" Gwen gave him her cell number and he sent her a text, so she'd have his. Then he grinned confidently. "I'll be seeing you."

Gwen stood there flabbergasted, and Chace vanished as suddenly as he'd appeared. Okay, so she had a plan. She'll go on this date and see how it turns out. Then she'll go on a second date with David, that's only if she ever had a chance in hell to say one word to him. However, Gwen was well enough prepared. Being a New Yorker was about taking risks and having two separate dates was a risk she was going to take. She was ahead of herself now, her brain not fully matured beyond her naivete. But all teenagers go through drastic measures in their life, even heavy-handed ones. She could probably give this a try. No worries. But Gwen still pestered, her mind once again drifting back to Bianca.

As soon as they were in the cab, Susan unloaded on the other dinner guests.

"You cannot believe how conceited they were," Susan groused. "I get the feeling they didn't even like each other."

"I thought you enjoyed yourself," Gwen replied, a little surprised.

"Yeah right," Susan scoffed. "I was only there to ask questions about the court case, that's it. And that Neal Walworth treated me like I was beholden to him. The mighty lawyer who tipped off a humble reporter to make himself look good. So I had to reel him in about the details of the trail, then bam! I'm continuing part two on the Bernstein court trail. Let me tell you somethin', baby doll, don't ever suck up to the rich. They're as fake as a three-dollar bill."

Gwen looked out the window, pondering about her own evening. "I don't know...Bianca doesn't seem so bad."

◆ ✳ ✳

THE RULES OF DATING

Gwen paced around the room, rummaging through her closet. The beating of her heart was full of anticipation. She fell into the pile of clothes, feeling a sensational rush of ecstasy. She was going on a date with the Senior prince of Hamilton Academy. She embellished in a daydream, imagining herself riding on a white carriage fastened to a train of three white horses, galloping through the streets of the crystalline city. Has fantasy ever become a reality for her? Not in a lifetime. Though, Gwen's relationships with boys weren't always an easy breeze.

Back in North Carolina, during freshman year, Gwen had been obsessed with a junior boy in her social studies class named Jimmy. He was one of those East Statesville skater boys who would hang around the local plaza mart. Gwen walked home from school every day just to get a glimpse of him. He was six'two, had brown bangs over his dark eyes, and a lean athletic build. She'd thought he was the sexiest boy she'd ever seen.

Jimmy finally approached her in the cafeteria, asking her to meet him at the football field on Friday. The football field was notorious for its make-out spots. Gwen was only fourteen at the time, not clearly knowing what his intentions were. So she went with her heart without using her head.

Gwen sat with him at the stadium, feeling fidgety. She thought she could break the tension by starting a conversation, though she can tell by the look in his eye, he wanted to do more than just talking. Then after a quiet interlude, Jimmy swiftly pulled her lips to his. Something just didn't feel right. The way they were kissing each other was like putting lips to an ice cream cone. Although she didn't have that much experience kissing boys, at least she got to share it with Jimmy. After their uneventful make-out session, he invited her to the movies the following Saturday. Gwen was having her first bouts of puppy love and it was hard for her to pull out of it.

Jimmy was sweet, generous, attentive to her needs, and had the potential to be the perfect boyfriend. But as they always say: the Gemini has two sides.

Gwen was beginning to see the signs the week after. She was seeing less and less of him, never calling her phone or acknowledging her in the hallways at school. And then there was the inevitable.

Jimmy met up with her after school, but he was not so eager to show his graciousness.

"Gwen, uh, I don't think this is working out," he said, dismissively.

Gwen took the breakup hard, crying for three whole days straight. In the back of her mind, she had the slightest curiosity to walk over to the football field. She'd came to discover Jimmy was kissing another girl. She was obviously much older and well-developed, and, by the way she was kissing him, she was much more experienced too.

Gwen felt her world shattering, yet the pains of freshman year was a lesson learned. Now that she transited into a new life, Gwen wondered if her hopes were getting too high. But she remained optimistic. This was going to be her first date in The Big Apple.

Gwen's cellphone rang. She hopped up from the floor and checked the caller ID. Maxine. Gwen gave out a wary sigh. If there was any crisis involving boys, Maxine was the girl of the hour. Why would she call at a time like this?

Gwen briskly clicked on the phone. "Hey, Maxine."

"Just wanted to see how things are going," she said slyly.

"I'm so nervous I'm not even dressed yet."

"Want me to give you some pointers?"

Gwen checked her watch. "I really don't have the time."

"Come on. You can't impress a guy like Chace Fairbanks alone, can you?"

"I'll just see how the evening goes. I'll call you later about it, okay."

"Keep me posted, doll. Good luck!"

Gwen clicked off the phone just as the doorbell rang, sending a cold chill down her spine.

"Gwen," Susan called in singsong voice. "Your date's here."

"I'll be out in a minute!" she called through the door.

Gwen continued tearing through her closet, more urgently this time, until she saw the dress she wanted to wear. Her aunt Linda had given it to her two years ago as a Christmas present. Susan said that the dress was too mature on Gwen, even though it was a simple gray knee-length sleeveless silk sheath with an additional light green shawl. Susan insisted Gwen to be a bit older before she wore it since Gwen was thirteen at the time. Now, Gwen suddenly knew it was the perfect time to wear it. With one glance at the clock, she slipped on the dress and put her hair up in messy bun. Gwen looked into the mirror, amazed how the silver-gray dress brought out her eyes more. The eyes Chace seemed so enchanted by.

Gwen draped the shawl around her shoulders, took a deep breath and walked out to the living room. It was just like that scene from *She's All That* except there weren't any stairs to fall on, thankfully. Susan was overjoyed. At first, she'd been doubtful Gwen would ever wear the dress, but she was delighted at how the sheath structure fit her perfectly. Chace, on the other hand, couldn't take his eyes off her.

Susan was squealing like an overexcited schoolgirl, much to Gwen's annoyance. "You have a splendid time!"

Gwen waved her mother goodbye as she and Chace made their way to the limo outside. Yes, a limo. The second time she got to ride a limo on her first REAL date. Gwen leaned against the window, taking in the New York City lights. She felt Chace's hand touch hers. Something magical was happening in the air.

"Beautiful, isn't it?" Chace said, gazing at Gwen.

She gazed back over at Chace, seeing how his dark blue eyes sparkled. "It sure is."

"I meant the dress," Chace retorted smoothly. "You look mighty fine."

Gwen felt like kissing him but restrained herself, knowing that wouldn't be ladylike. Certainly not in the first minute of the first date. "So where are we going this evening?"

"Roxelle's. It's one of my favorite restaurants."

"Sounds like a strip club," Gwen giggled, embarrassed by her own words.

Chace laughed wholeheartedly. "Trust me, it's the fanciest place in town."

The place was fancy all right. It had a sort of grand castle entrance with a crystal chandelier suspended from the vaulted ceiling. The gold-plated walls shone around the jeweled statue water fountains, the carpet thick and lush over the Mediterranean tiles. The place had a trans-Atlantic atmosphere that simply felt luxurious. Even the guests were dressed elegantly, their formal wear seemed straight off the runway, in contrast to Gwen's simple gray dress. But this wasn't the path Chace was heading to.

Gwen followed him farther back, into a dimly lit room decorated with clouds of cigarette smoke. Gwen coughed in the haze, confused by this dive hidden behind the glitz of the other restaurant. This place was like some seedy casino bar. The barflies were sad- looking middle-aged men slumped over the counter and rowdy twenty-something guys who catcalled at the scantily clad waitresses while playing their round of drinking games. Gwen's heart sank. Chace was crazy to think that this place would be a good first date venue.

Chace snapped his fingers and pointed to an empty booth. "My favorite spot. Let's go grab it."

Gwen sat stiffly in the chrome-leather booth, not saying a word. Chace sat close beside her.

"What's the matter, babe?" Chace said, holding Gwen's hand.

"Nothing. I'm doing just fine," Gwen responded, smiling through her gritted teeth.

One of the waitresses sashayed over to the table in her halter top and high-waisted shorts. She leered openly at Chace, ignoring Gwen. "What'll it be, sexy?" she said seductively.

Chace gave her a charming smile. "Gin with a splash of tonic, use the big glass and save yourself another trip in five minutes."

Geez, Gwen thought. *Drink much?*

"And bring us a couple of menus, we'll be ordering dinner tonight. Gwen, what would you like to drink?"

"Orange juice," Gwen blurted out nervously.

The waitress didn't bother to hide her laugh. "Your order will be right up, sir." With an alluring wink, the waitress turned, giving Chace a full view of her butt.

Gwen sank in her seat, a bit embarrassed. Was Chace flirting with the waitress? What was this place?

Not a second too soon, the drinks and menus came. Chace downed half of his gin while Gwen was deciding and requested another drink when the waitress returned for their meal order. Finally, he had Gwen's full attention. "So what subject will be discussing? School perhaps?"

"We all know about that," Gwen quipped.

Chace laughed as he finished his drink. "Yeah, you definitely don't want to deal with those jerks after hours." He waved over at a nearby waitress. "Hey, can you give me some apple schnapps? My mouth is a bit bitter."

Gwen's smile disappeared. "Are you even allowed to drink?"

"It's okay. I'm a regular here." The schnapps arrived with his gin and tonic. Chace downed the schnapps in one shot and chased it with a swig of gin. "Woo! That hits the spot!" He howled.

Gwen stared at him in disappointment. How could someone get drunk on their first date? It was something straight out of some train wreck reality TV show.

When the food arrived, Chace raised his glass, which was again filled with gin. "Here's to a wonderful date," he said, slurring a bit.

Yeah, right. Gwen tried not to roll her eyes.

She ate her food, not even bothering to say two words to him.

"Why so quiet, babe?" Chace said, giving her a goofy grin.

"Can we just go home?" Gwen sighed, feeling a little annoyed and a lot disappointed.

"All right. But first, I would be honored to show you my house."

Gwen agreed, mostly because she was eager to get out of there.

Back in the limo, she was relieved to be free of the suffocating smoky aroma and rolled down the window to enjoy the late-summer night air. Gwen stared out the window, vacantly this time, no longer so enamored by the city lights. She could feel Chace rub up against her, his alcohol-soaked breath on her cheek.

Chace traced his finger up her leg. "Have I told you how beautiful you are tonight?"

"Yes, more than once," Gwen said, annoyed, although she kept a smile on her face to keep the vibe friendly, despite her growing discomfort.

"Here we are."

The limo stopped in front of a four-story slate-gray townhouse on an insanely posh street. Chace stepped out, trying to keep his composure as he struggled to open Gwen's door and entered the house. Gwen sighed wearily, predicting how this date would end. Should she just ditch now? She knew it would be rude to bail and take off like that, but what were the options at this point? This guy was literately drunk off his feet. However, Gwen was a trooper. All she had to do was endure this for a few extra minutes while he lurched around the house. He'd probably pass out as soon as he found a couch anyway and she could leave without a fuss. Gwen was beginning to like Chace, she really did, but this was ridiculous.

The inside of the townhouse was wide and long, much bigger than Maxine's penthouse. Amazed by the swanky décor of the home, Gwen wandered into the study room full of Hollywood memorabilia and century-old photographs.

"My parents aren't home," Chace said, snickering.

Gwen ignored him and continued to gaze at the items displayed around the room. She picked up a wedding photo of Douglas Fairbanks Jr. and Joan Crawford, touching the gold-steel edges of the picture frame. With Gwen's vast knowledge of the Hollywood golden age, the marriage was quite short-lived.

Suddenly, she felt Chace's hands slide down to her hips.

"Come on. I have a surprise for you," he whispered in her ear.

Gwen flinched at the foul stench of alcohol in his breath. She didn't know whether this was a romantic gesture or a sleazy come-on, but she went anyway.

Gwen followed Chace into his bedroom, not surprised to see how utterly messy it was, even though he probably had twenty housekeepers to clean it.

Gwen politely sat on the bed, trying to hide her uneasiness.

He's like any other boy all right, Gwen thought. *It's Statesville all over again.*

Chace kissed her on the cheek, running his fingers through her hair. He whispered, "Wait," and vanished through the door in the room. Gwen contemplated whether or not if she should make a run for it now. No, wait, she just had to see what this "surprise" was. If it was something idiotic, there was her chance.

Gwen held her cellphone, ready to call a taxi or her mom, if need be. Then she heard steps from behind her. Gwen turned around. Her eyes grew big.

"Ta-da."

Chace was full buck naked, with a dopey smirk on his face. He staggered over to the bed, his eyelids slightly drooping. Gwen sat there, shell-shocked. She had never seen a boy naked in her life and it was weird how it was happening now. On her first real date, no less.

Chace leaned toward her, letting her hair down. He plopped down next to her, rubbing his chest against her arm; she heard his heart beating rapidly. "Come here, I know you want it."

Suddenly, Gwen no longer cared if he thought her rude. "Chace, you're drunk," she said sternly.

"I know you waited for this for the longest time—"

"I said get off!" Gwen elbowed him in the abdomen, knocking him to the floor. Although, she was concerned about his well-being, Gwen brushed it off and headed for the door.

"Wait, Gwen...Where are you going?" Chace moaned, holding his stomach.

Gwen stared down at him with pity, still looking at his body, which was perfection in every way, yet completely unappealing to her. "I'm going home, Chace. What I should've done a long time ago."

"You gonna call me tomorrow?"

She left, without saying a word. Once Gwen made a run for it outside, she breathed a sigh of relief as if letting go of the whole sordid incident.

A taxi cab drove near the sidewalk and Gwen hopped in, resting her head against the window, closing her eyes shut. Now she knew what kind of "baggage" Bianca carried from her relationship with Chace. How could she even deal with it? Bianca had warned her of what was to come. And she'd learned it the hard way. Sure, everybody had their off days but how many off days can a person take? It was self-sabotage before her eyes.
Gwen should've listened to Bianca, talked to her longer, really respected what the other girl was trying to say. And maybe, just maybe, she could've saved herself from this horrible night.

J. D. Fitzgerald

◆ ✳ ✳

CLEAR BLUE SATURDAY

Gwen made her way to the Madame Lasvar building in SoHo, mainly so she could avoid spending a lazy Saturday afternoon at home. And plus, she'd do almost anything to forget that humiliating date with Chace last night.

Trust me, I'll be the perfect gentlemen. His awful words rang through her head. He hadn't been anything like a gentleman after those few cocktails.

Shaking off her negative ruminations, Gwen got out of the cab and started pacing the sidewalk. A crowd of pedestrians burst out onto the pavement, like a stampede of buffaloes escaping from a pen. The swarm of tourists thinned out for Gwen to break free as she strolled across the street. She had a chance to gaze at a group of young women passing her way, each of them dressed in designer wear. She could've sworn she'd seen some of the girls from school. But then Gwen realized, they were just other models traveling off to their go-sees, sporting the same bored expressions they usually did at their photo shoots.

They must really hate their jobs, Gwen thought.

Some gave Gwen disgusted looks, rudely bumping their shoulders into her, which was odd considering these were women in their early to mid-twenties. Gwen didn't understand why they were being so hostile until she noticed her worn-out Mickey Mouse T-shirt, faded-out jeans and two-year-old sneakers. Gwen just simply didn't feel like dressing up today. However, it wasn't just her appearance. It was more so her age-range, considering how the older models looked at her as if she was some hot young nubile newcomer, threatening to take away their spotlight. Competition seems to be a part of these girls' lives, and Gwen kind of felt sorry for them.

Finally, she went inside the Madame Lasvar building.

The atmosphere was, of course, hectic. The set directors were putting up props and lights, fashion coordinators were having a heated discussion with the studio photographer, makeup artists were setting up suitcases of makeup kits, and the rest of the crew were running around trying to keep the place functioning. Gwen stepped into a circus-level of proportions.

A tall, white-haired middle-aged man in dark sunglasses approached Gwen with a stern, strict smile. He had a tall, slim frame and his outfit was paired in a turtleneck, blazer, and slacks, all matched in black. His entire aura was a contrived air of mystery.

"Good afternoon, Mrs. Stevenson. I'm Jay French, and welcome to our domain." He kept his stern smile as he examined Gwen's outfit. "Let's freshen you up."

With a snap of his fingers, Jay's entourage ambushed Gwen, escorting her off to the dressing room.

And now, here she was, being powdered up with far too much makeup. Was she even allowed to wear red lipstick? The wardrobe was the worst part though. She was forced to wear a short black tight latex dress that was almost suffocating, along with towering thigh-high boots and fishnet stockings labeled by Victoria's Secret. This was *degrading.* She looked like a common prostitute.

She reminded herself, there was a reason she agreed to do this: to see just how horrible the fashion industry could be. If only she had a pen and pad to write down the many crimes they committed. Their first offense: dressing a not yet sixteen-year-old as a sex worker. All she had to do was give Vera a call and meet her over at Lupe's East L.A. Restaurant if things went too far. It was her perfect escape plan.

When she finally got out of the dressing room, a young woman with a curtain of black hair stood in front of her, dressed in a white one shoulder knee-length dress. Her exotic Caribbean-island features proposed the notion that she was more than just a catalog model.

"Hello there! I'm Saleshia Roberts," she said in a nasal tone of voice. "First, before we begin shooting, I'd like to give you a little tour of how things go around here."

Gwen resisted her eyes from rolling, copying the same fake smile the model was sporting.

The so-called tour only lasted no more than five minutes but seemed so much longer. Gwen could feel the blisters developing around the heel of her pointy boots. God, it was excruciating.

Then, it was time for the photo shoot.

Saleshia shifted around and gave her a dainty handshake. "Good luck." She winked, flashing her toothpaste-commercial smile as she floated away with her entourage.

All looks but no personality, Gwen jested thoughtfully.

Then things started to get really unpleasant. Gwen was placed in the most uncompromising pose, laid straight down in front of the camera. The boisterous howls of the circulator fan were ringing in her ears with strands of her hair flinging across her face. Her knee was bent up, exposing certain parts of her thigh almost to her nether-regions, while the photographer barked orders in a Scandinavian accent. Too bad she didn't know what the hell he was saying.

After just one photo shoot, Gwen was already agitated. The lights were almost blinding, the obnoxious photographer was shouting out incomprehensible tasks, and the assembled crowd of advisers was looking on condescendingly, writing notes. Enough! This was her breaking point.

Right in the middle of the shoot, Gwen got up, took off the boots, and flung the feet-swelling contraptions across the room.

"Young lady, what do you think you're doing!" Jay French huffed with his arms crossed.

Gwen continued to the dressing room and grabbed her battered black sneakers. Just as she was about to exit, Jay halted her.

"Young lady, I'm talking to you."

Gwen looked him in the eye. "Thank you for your time, Mr. French, but just to let you know, this is totally not what I signed up for." Gwen walked past him to the exit door, leaving the man dumbfounded.

Down in the elevator and out the front door, Gwen smelled the air of good weather; although a bit more polluted, it still reminded Gwen of the clear blue days of North Carolina. She instantly dialed Vera's number, in need of her company.

"Yes, I got here as soon as you called," Vera answered. "Wanting to be saved from the fashion industry?"

"I escaped when I had the chance. Can we just meet up at Lupe's."

"No problem." Vera paused. "But I have a surprise in store for you."

"Oh no, not that," Gwen moaned, not particularly prepared for the unexpected.

"Aw cheer up, mountain girl. You'll love me for it."

Grabbing the nearest city bus, Gwen arrived at Lupe's a short time later. Inside the restaurant, she froze, her eyes growing wide.

David Henderson, the co-star of her dreams, sat at the last table booth. He lifts his head and gazed at Gwen. There was a twinkle in his eye and she saw he had a blush of red over his cheeks.

Gwen kept her voice from fluttering. "Hi."

"Hi." David's face illuminated beautifully in the sunlight, bringing out the complexion of his skin. She felt like reaching out to him and entering his embrace one more time.

The butterflies in Gwen's stomach was swarming up again and she reached her hand to quell them. When she touched the latex rubbery fabric of her abdomen, she noticed she was still wearing the ridiculous dominatrix dress from the fashion shoot. With tennis shoes this time.

"Don't mind the outfit," Gwen said, wrapping her arms around herself timidly. "I was doing an... experiment."

"No, it's okay. I...like it," David complimented bashfully. "Do you wanna grab a bite to eat?"

Gwen beamed. "Sure! But isn't Vera joining us?"

"She got tied up with a couple of things. So, we'll probably see her later."

"Right," Gwen said, not fooled by Vera's sudden disappearance.

Her prayers have been answered. Honey-brown-eyed David with his adorable smile to brighten up her day. Vera witnessed the sizzling chemistry from the movie shoot, grasping the situation to fulfill her role as matchmaker. She knew exactly what she was doing when she played her cards right. Even Maxine would be impressed.

Sitting by the window, over cheese-glazed nachos, Gwen reveled in how comfortable and safe she felt around David. It was just like being on a date. *Or is it a date, in fact?* She was having lunch with the guy she'd locked lips for the first time, the first time she ever had any contact with him by the way, so as far as she knows, this was, officially, a date.

Their conversation didn't completely take off at first. From each quiet beat, they replied in short sentences.

"How are you?" David asked reticently.

"Fine," Gwen answered back.

Then stop.

Gwen's debilitating social ineptness was graveling at her peak. What's there to say to him? There was a connection, unfortunately, Gwen was too hesitant to get ahead of muddled communication. Though her mind begin to wonder. What was in that notebook of his? Therefore, Gwen found a way to utilize her social skills. "What do you like to write?"

David's eyes lit up at her curiosity. "Poetry."

Gwen was piqued with interest. "Wow, really? When did you start writing poetry?"

"I started when I was eleven." David took a moment. "The first poem I ever wrote was kind of personal to me but...do you mind if I read a verse to you?"

Gwen's heart skipped a beat. "Sure, I would love to hear it!"

David closed his eyes, counting back in memory. After quiet observation, he opened his eyes and recited the words.

Woman in red,

You left me in

dread,

Woman in red,

Will my conscious be

read?

Woman in read,

I bestilled my soul in

wonder, But why am I left in

somber?

Woman in red

Oh, Woman in red

You rip the hearts of men,

And you leave them...dead

Gwen was marveled by his passion. *This guy was amazing.* "You wrote that when you was eleven?

"I was a weird kid," David chuckled lightly.

"Wow. How did you come up with that poem?"

"It's a long story." David turned away, letting the memory sink in.

"I didn't mean to..."

"It's okay," David reassured. "It's very painful to talk about, but I think I'm comfortable to tell you."

"It's alright. I'll just listen."

"Well, the poem is about my mother."

Gwen was intrigued. "It sounds so...intricate."

"The stinger was, I caught my mom kissing another man while I was peeking out the window. I was only five years old."

David adjusted himself, engraved in his thoughts. It wasn't the easiest subject to discuss, but he was touched by Gwen's sincerity, being able to freely express his feelings.

He let out a sharp breath. "Experiencing that was such a blur. Though, I think what really got me, was when the day my mom left. It was something I couldn't get over and it sort of haunted me ever since then. But I found a way to break the vessel. By writing about it."

Gwen observed at how deeply he told his story. She knew how it felt to be abandoned by a parent at a young age and even as Gwen got older, the wounds of her heartbreak were still fresh, holding on to the pain of handling her dad's addiction. Though as a way to cope with her troubled past, Gwen decided to let it be known and heard within in her words. She saw how David just revealed himself, revealed his mind, body, and soul from just how he expressed the words in his poem. She only met this guy once and she felt safe to tell him about her afflictions.

"I guess it's my turn now." Gwen held her breath and she looked up at David; his eyes were sympathetic and direct. His ears were open, and he was ready to listen. "My father is an alcoholic. He'd have these on and off phases of being drunk and sober, but once he starts drinking, it was all happening too fast. He had his share of affairs too, being gone from hours of the night. I can just remember how epic my mom and dad's fights were but somehow, she stuck by him. My mom was amazing. We'd been through it together, so I couldn't blame her, but still I felt like she could fix it somehow. At that time, I blamed her and then myself, because I felt I wasn't good enough. I had such a low self- esteem and it kind of went on for a while. Now that I'm older, I understand. She had no choice but to leave him. Finally, I realized the only person responsible, was my dad." Gwen stared outside the window. She squinted real hard, struggling for the tears to not fall down; she couldn't let it get to her. "He's like a stranger to me. I barely think about him. Maybe it's easier to forget all the hurt he's caused. Maybe that's why my mom moved. Staying in Statesville was just too painful for her, and, she had to seize every opportunity for us to live a better life."

David held Gwen's hand. "Parents do disappoint us, there's no getting around that."

Gwen held back tight, trying to keep her voice from trembling. "Yeah."

"You're a special girl, Gwen. I mean I just met you, but you have a good heart."

"So do you."

They gazed into each other's eyes for a moment. Their hands were connected, stimulated by the touch, reaching into their souls. Gwen wasn't sure if she'd ever met a boy like David before; he was truly one of a kind. Sensitive, thoughtful, artistic. Once Gwen looked into David's brown eyes, she knew this was her Holden Caulfield, the guy who was not confined by what society thought of him. She wished the minute could go on longer.

Reluctantly Gwen stood up, not wanting to go too soon. "I have to go. It was really nice talking to you."

David stood with her. "Before you go, Vera thought it would be cool if you could go with us to the Five and Dime tonight. Her sister's band is performing."

"I will totally be there," Gwen said excitedly. "I'll give Vera a call to get the details."

Gwen turned. But stopped. She faced David again, feeling as if she forgot something. She slowly wrapped her arms around him and enjoyed his embrace, smelling his clean curls and masculine scent. She would give anything to kiss him at this moment, though it would be best to save it for the right time.

"Goodbye, David...I'll be seeing you."

J. D. Fitzgerald

◆

* *

EVERY GIRL'S DREAM. OR WHATEVER

Kyle sat at the rocking chair, her eyes glued to the antique grandfather clock. She waited, impatiently, for the limo to arrive. She wasn't exactly thrilled about attending the Kiss the Stars charity ball. She wasn't particularly excited about going with Jeremy Fletcher either. Then... why was she so nervous? This was the first time in her life that a boy has invited her to a party. Yes, he was attractive but with Jeremy, once the conversation started, it fell dead on its feet, halted by uninteresting topics like sports, card playing, body-building, skiing, surfing, etc. Then whenever her topics of interest came up, he'd have this bored glazed-over expression, changing the subject and not bothering to hide his own lack of interest.

Tonight, he wasn't a date, he was...an escort. Because if he was a date, he would have to at least try to impress her in some way. On the other hand, what was taking so long with the limo?

Kyle went to the study to take a look in the mirror beside the tall flower vase. When she first applied makeup, it kind of felt...good. Previously, she had been totally caught up in her mother's opinions of beauty—the whole "less is more" agenda—but now she thought, a little makeup couldn't possibly hurt.

Thinking of all those times she was just a Plain Jane, hiding in her book, she knew she could've simply spread her wings and showed the true beauty of herself but had made the decision to never stoop down to Bianca's or any of those girls' level. However, tonight was different. She was going to show everyone how capable and confident she was— inside and out.

She looked womanly in the blue dress Maxine gave her. The satin bodice clung to her torso and the hem draped down above the knees, showing off her shapely legs. Kyle felt like a rose in bloom, the ugly duckling turned into a swan, although she was no Cinderella and she wasn't looking for a Prince Charming to save her. She was just a girl trying to prove herself.

Kyle heard the doorbell ring. Jeremy Fletcher, the furthest thing imaginable from a prince, had arrived.

She walked into the living room, where her parents were charmed by Jeremy. Or at least pretending to be. William and Patricia wouldn't be amused by someone whose only topics were sports and beer.

"You got yourself a fine catch here," her father said in his usual loud boom. She suspected he was lying, no one could consider the snore-inducing Jeremy a catch, even without their lack of chemistry.

Patricia stood up and gave Kyle a firm hug. "You be back no later than twelve-thirty." Patricia smoothed the back of her daughter's dress. "You look beautiful. Enjoy yourself."

When Kyle stepped onto the sidewalk, she was shocked to learn there was no limo. Not that she was a high-maintenance girl, but judging from Jeremy's financial background, she hadn't expected he'd be driving a beat-up silver Chevy.

Jeremy spread his arms with a flourish, as if to show the beauty of the car, despite its decrepit appearance. "This is my grandfather's 1962 Chevy. Don't worry, it drives well. We just spent so many years getting it to run, we haven't had time to work on the cosmetic stuff."

It took Kyle a moment. "I...It will be an honor to ride in your grandfather's Chevy."

Jeremy put on a lopsided grin and opened her door ceremoniously. "I like your spirit."

The car arrived at the Waldorf Astoria without a hitch, not a traffic jam in sight. Suddenly, the consummate gentleman, Jeremy gave the keys to the valet and came around to open the door for Kyle; for the first time, she felt like a princess going to the royal ball. This was her first party ever and she never felt this special.

Jeremy took her arm and escorted Kyle through the crowd of people and into the hotel. Everybody was still in awe of her transformation. Some in satisfaction. Some in scorn. Though, there was one girl whose envy defeated them all.

Bianca Walworth, dressed in a black evening dress, stood regally in her usual superior stance, but the look on her face was in deep concern, almost regretful.

She walked up to Kyle, her hands folded in front. "I would like to apologize."

Kyle was baffled. "Apologize?"

"I know it's weird that I'm approaching you this way, it's just...my jealously can get the best of me sometimes."

"I see," Kyle said in an acerbic tone.

"Well, screw the rules about the whole extra-curricular activities thing, I'm sure we can get that arranged somehow."

"Wait, are suggesting...I get to join...?"

Bianca smiled gracefully. "I hereby declare you an honorary member. Please take a moment to meet and greet with your fellow comrades by the dining area. I'm sure they'll enjoy your company."

Bianca waltzed away, leaving Kyle quite perplexed. Did she take happy pills in a week's span of time? Why the sudden change of heart? For the two years Kyle had spent in Hamilton, Bianca Walworth was a girl of mystery. But in life, there is always more questions than answers, so it was best to enjoy her time here.

"Ready to set the night ablaze, m'lady," Jeremy said as he wrapped his arm around her waist.

Kyle didn't say anything back. She stopped, her mind racing off. She had to do this sooner or later. She looked at Jeremy for a moment. "Jeremy, I think it's best if we don't date anymore."

Jeremy's smile disappeared. "Did I do something wrong?"

"No," Kyle said, surprised at how calm and sincere she was. At first, she'd looked at Jeremy like the typical jock he seemed to be, though right now, she saw him as a sad little boy getting his heart broken, so she let him down gently. "I don't want to lead you on any further...It's like I'm going in one direction and you're in the other. I'm sorry, Jeremy. There's just no way it'll ever work."

"Yeah...Too bad you're hot, though."

She threw her head back, with a simple laugh. "You're such a charmer."

Kyle left him with a smile and went on to find her collective peers. The honor society members graciously let her join their little circle by the dining area. Chatting with intellectuals such as herself, she proudly presented her interests in the spotlight.

Her destiny solidified.

J. D. Fitzgerald

TONIGHT, TONIGHT

Gwen paced around the room, her thoughts tangled in a tightrope. She began her pre-special event ritual: trying on various outfits while listening to her Lana Del Rey CD. This time it was a night out at the Five and Dime, where Vera's sister Matilda was performing with her band, the Loco Bitches. Gwen opened the closet door but then halted, seeing the rows of new designer wear Maxine had bought for her. Old clothes were buried within the fabrics of silver, gold, and lame. Old shoes, mostly sneakers were replaced with Jimmy Choos and Manolo Blahniks. It wasn't as if following the Hamilton Academy dress code was mandatory, but for the sake of Gwen's morality, she was heading pretty close to the brink of an identity crisis.

She grabbed an arm full of the expensive wardrobe and threw them on the floor. Now, the words of what her mother said suddenly registered. *Don't ever suck up to the rich.*

Soon, Gwen heard her cellphone buzzing on the dresser. She clicked it on and saw Maxine's text glowing on the screen:

Party at Waldorf Astoria. Please be there!

She clicked the phone off. *Sorry, Maxine. I already made up my mind.*

Gwen sat down and gazed at the mirror. She appreciated Maxine's contribution to changing her image, but the aftereffect was almost deceitful. Frazzled by Hamilton's perception of high school, Gwen seem to lose her will to follow her own path. She wasn't allowed to be herself and it was troubling to see that this was the way to live. She was nothing more than a simple country girl from North Carolina, accepting who she was and chose to be.

Her cellphone buzzed again. Gwen gave out a tired sigh. *I'm not going, Maxine.* She checked the caller ID. Oh, it was Chace. It was the tenth time he'd called but Gwen couldn't bring herself to hear his voice. The events from the date from hell kept replaying in her head, it was hard to erase her disdain. Therefore, seeing Chace's name pop up on her phone every six seconds didn't help matters. She knew she had to answer sooner or later; somewhere down the line, there had to be explanation for his unpredictable behavior those few nights ago. One of the basic skills of growing up was facing a problem and fixing it. But maybe she could put it off just a little bit longer.

Instead, she gave Vera a call. Finally, picking out her attire for the evening, Gwen settled on a *Powerpuff Girls* T-shirt she'd had and loved since the seventh grade, now showing just a little tiny bit of midriff, with a denim jacket, the plaid green skirt she'd worn on her first day of school, the fishnet stockings from that horrendous fashion shoot, and last but not least, her trustworthy skater shoes. Each pair of clothing was like a fashion collage of her first few weeks in New York, a well-deserved badge of honor.

She took a satisfied look in the mirror, then headed out to the city.

Gwen met Vera, sitting on the bench, looking bored and impatient in the nearby subway district. She was relieved when she caught sight of Gwen entering the station.

"Thank god, you're here. The subway was insanely crowded. It's finally cleared out in the nick of time." Vera was wearing high-waisted shorts paired up in white-striped purple tights with a large black Nirvana T-shirt tied to the waist, her short brown hair styled up in a new wave hawk.

"You look great, Vera," Gwen complimented.

"Same to you, Powerpuff Girl. I like the threads. You ready to hightail on out to Brooklynville?"

"Don't mind if I do."

The subway was jam-packed, even more so than the ride to Coney Island. You had your weirdos, your college students, and your stage and band performers all in one car. Saturday nights were indeed the busiest nights.

The two girls breathed a sigh of fresh air once they made it to Brooklyn, disembarking in Williamsburg, the go-to hotspot for hipsters and aspiring artists, and just a few blocks down the street, they found where the Five and Dime was located, just around the corner.

On the way to the entrance door, Gwen had to endure an onslaught of smoke and noise, much like she had experienced on her one and only date with Chace. Her eyes adjusted to the dim lighting of neon blue, illuminating the place in a cool watery texture. It was quite sophisticated, though, with an alternative touch. Calm and laid-back, just her kind of atmosphere.

They spotted Mona sitting at a table near the stage; she immediately waved them over. She was the spitting image of Joan Jett, fashioned in a black wife beater, cut-off gloves, and a short leather skirt. Mona never looked any better.

She lifted up her glass of beer to greet the girls. "Glad you guys could make it."

"Hey, how did you get that beer?" Vera interrogated playfully as she and Gwen joined Mona. "You haven't been flirting with the bartender, have you?"

"No," Mona chuckled. "I borrowed your sister's ID. We talked for a while earlier and she hooked me up, because, we look so much alike. I mean, even our names kind of sound similar, right? Matilda, Mona. I got it all in place, babe."

Vera arched an eyebrow. "You are very clever, my girl. I think you and my sister will get along *pretty* well. Where is she, by the way?"

"She's at the Eaglewave, prepping up for the show. More importantly, Gwen, a gentleman is waiting for you."

Gwen traced her eyes over at the front row and saw David dressed in a tuxedo, two sizes too big, sitting at a table by the corner, waiting patiently. She walked over, a cold rush was tingling inside her.

"Hi," Gwen greeted softly.

David anxiously perked up in his chair. "Hey."

Gwen sat down with a warm smile on her face. "I wanted to thank you and Vera again for inviting me. It's a relief to be around normal people for a change."

"Yeah. It's my favorite place to unwind. I'd come here every day if I can."

Gwen locked eyes with David. "You look very handsome."

The redness around David's cheeks glowed. "Thanks."

Their hands touched accidentally but Gwen recoiled, her own cheeks blushing.

The doors suddenly opened, grabbing everybody's attention. A loud, raspy voice echoed through the club.

"Wassup, rockers!"

A woman, who looked to be in her early twenties, came strolling in the entrance door. There was exotic middle-eastern features under her goth makeup, her hair sported up in a teased up bob, and she was dressed in a sexually garish catsuit, the tight layer of leather hugging her slim figure. She was gallant with the club patrons as they clapped and cheered, giving the vibe that the young woman was a regular here. From the look of her stagy introduction, it didn't take long for Gwen to figure out that this must be Matilda.

In contrast, Vera just sat in her seat, letting her sister soak in all the attention. Despite their similar physical features, Matilda's vivacious energy was an opposition to Vera's more subtle social approach.

Matilda soon broke away from her adoring posse and walked over to the table while Gwen was keeping an eye on this intriguing character.

Matilda waltzed up to Vera. "Seems like you brought your little friends to my show," she said in a primly tone.

Vera gave off a smirk. "They wouldn't miss it for the world. And just because they're a few years younger than you, doesn't make them little."

"Woah, back up little sis, just makin' conversation."

Gwen assumed there was tension in the air but then she realized, this was just playful banter between the two sisters. The girls had a weird sense humor that was a little antagonistic but mostly a natural sort of sibling thing.

It was three minutes when one of Matilda's bandmates arrived, a girl dressed in the same leather gear with purple hair shaped up in an electric-spiked Mohawk, was having small talk with the bartender. Matilda motioned her to join in at the table.

"Hey, long-lost twin," Matilda said to Mona, giving her a secret wink.

Mona just giggled to herself, taking a swig of her beer as a nod to her gratitude.

Matilda leaned over beside Gwen. "And you must be Gwen. Like your outfit. *Powerpuff Girls,* huh?" she wisecracked.

Gwen laughed lightly, pointing to her chest. "That's what it says on the label," she chirped.

Matilda then turned her attention toward David. "Davy, my man! Glad you dressed up for the occasion, but in a place like this, tuxedos aren't allowed, buddy boy."

David chuckled. "I'll keep that in mind."

As she arrived at the table, Mohawk girl whispered in Matilda's ear. Her joyful nature was fading into slight irritation, not liking what was being whispered to her. She stood up from the table and tapped a spoon on her glass.

"Okay, guys, I'm sorry to announce that our lead guitarist Chrissy has bailed out on us, since she is too involved with her personal problems to show up these days. I'm afraid we can't play the songs on the list, it requires a guitar solo. What a bummer."

"Come on, Matilda, you got only fifteen minutes," Vera chided in. "Pick out someone from the audience to give it a try." She glanced at Mona, a sly smirk was spread across her face. "Or better yet, why won't you ask Mona to do the guitar solo?"

Mona's eyes widened, bemused by the suggestion. "Woah, Woah, Woah, now. Let's not get out of bounds here," she pleaded. Though once the idea persuaded her, she felt a sense of eagerness, yet with no experience on stage, her confidence crumbled into a deep hole of apprehension.

Matilda checked the time on her cell. "Okay, the love-in's over. Let's get this show on the road, ladies. You comin', girl?"

Mona glanced over at Gwen to send her nod of approval. Gwen projected her encouragement by raising two crossed fingers, which prompted Mona to snap out of her frozen state and join Matilda and Mohawk girl backstage. The spotlight was on, and she was at the verge of self-combustion.

Mona rested her head on the brown leather couch of the dressing room. Her nerves softened as she engaged in a friendly conversation with Mohawk girl. Her name was Nina Kisskill, who recently got back from Philadelphia a year ago. The two girls held a bonding session, discussing their favorite rock bands while studying their music notes. Although by first impression, inclined to Nina's razor-sharp veneer, she carried off a relaxed, chill manner.

"I don't know, I get the feeling that this was all set up," Mona assumed.

"Matilda said you were a safe bet," Nina explained. "So, I guess you're a part of the band."

"How so? Nobody has seen me play one string."

"Listen, just think of this as an experience," Nina reassured. "It's nothing permanent, that's entirely up to you. Hear my words, don't fret and stay focus. I'll give you some time to think about it."

When Nina left the room, Mona paced around nervously. She finally sat down and took a moment to compose herself. She was actually going on stage. Performing on stage. The rush was too much. Could she handle it? Handle what was in store at this moment? Thanks to Vera, it wasn't what she asked for but deep down inside, it was a blessing.

Matilda popped her head in the door. "Hey, what's up, girl?"

Mona held her arms together, feeling vulnerable and exposed. "I guess I'm having nervous knots. I've never really done this before."

Matilda knelled beside Mona and gave her a gentle pat on the back. "I have a couple of stage frights myself. But when you feel that jolt inside you, that rush of energy, the whole room will disappear. By the time you get on that stage, don't just play it for them, play it for you."

"Do you think I can do this?" Mona quivered, trying not to sound like a scared little girl.

"No, duh. You have it in you. When Vera showed me that video clip of you strumming your guitar. Man, it was like golden."

Mona blinked her eyes. "What video clip?"

Matilda winced. "Oops."

"Jesus, what's next?"

"Vera can be a very pushy girl, but she always means well. I got something to show you."

Matilda shuffled through the metal closet door, pulling out a guitar in the shape of an ax. Mona's jaw dropped. Never had she seen a guitar mold with such artistry and physicality. It looked ancient. Historically ancient.

"Circa 1987," Matilda so proudly announced. "Born and bred from the rock gods, whoever they may be."

Mona held the guitar. Blood was rushing from the impact of just grasping it in her hand.

"Are...are you giving it to me?" Mona asked with urgency.

"Maybe in another lifetime. But tonight, it's all yours. Let me show you how this baby works. You got to be real gentle with it. Go with the simple strokes, after that, go with your own pace."

Mona got the hang of handling the rhythm, being guided by the notes Matilda wrote for the song. Mona's stride and energy begin to pick up, taking the hook, servicing it as her own.

Then it was showtime.

When the band members were secluded, Mona panted swiftly. She held the guitar in her hand, the strap handle feeling heavy on her shoulders. At home, she would play her own guitar so freely and lively, feeling every rhythm and every melody, peeling away her emotions. Now at this moment, she was going to play on center stage and she didn't know what to do.

Matilda suddenly leaned close to her ear and whispered, "Make Momma proud, baby girl."

Soon, Mona felt a sense of warmth and security. Whatever the circumstances may be, someone would always have her back.

Mona followed the crew toward the stage, her fingers shaking with anticipation.

The announcer boomed through the intercom, "And now introducing, the Loco Bitches!"

A rush of adrenaline pumped into Mona's veins, blasting out all of her agitation. She fell into the music she was passionate about, and always wanted to play: Rock'n'roll. The band's songs had a mix heavy metal and electronica, which they mastered beautifully. Gwen and Vera headbanged in unison, pumped up by Mona's stage presence.

Mona's riff was so powerful that the whole world cheered in satisfaction. This wasn't in the comfort of her bedroom. She was in front of a live audience. Her dream coming true.

By the time the performance was over, Mona ran up to Gwen and Vera, overwhelmed but excited.

"You were amazing!" Gwen exclaimed.

Matilda put an arm around Mona's shoulder. "She could be quite the protégé."

Mona blinked at Matilda. "Portege? You're joking, right?"

"Let's have a little girl talk alone, shall we?"

Matilda whisked Mona away, giving Vera the opportunity to work her magic on Gwen and David.

Once the DJ started playing, Gwen jumped up excitedly. "Oh my gosh, I love this song!" She shyly looked over her shoulder. "Can somebody dance with me?"

Vera glanced at David and jerked her head toward Gwen, urging him to the dance floor. Gwen took off her jacket and twirled while holding David's hand. All she felt was euphoria, hearing the classical vocals and instrumental vibes of Electric Guest. As shy as she was, Gwen never thought she would burst out in front of a crowd of people, dancing her socks off. That magical feeling swayed within her surroundings, her soul bathing in the depths of serenity. This was her utopia.

Suddenly, the music slowed down into the soulful ballad of Alabama Shakes' "You Ain't Alone."

Gwen let David draw her close. She laid her cheek on his shoulder, shut her eyes, and exhaled. Gwen could hear his heartbeat grow faster, feeling his whole body quivering. She gazed into his eyes, trailing her fingers through his hair to calm him. On the other side, Vera gazed affectionately at the two, satisfied that her two best buddies were having the time of their life.

Gwen tilted her head, catching David's breath. He leaned down and softly touched his lips to hers; she again felt that familiar tingle. This time, there was no camera rolling. Their kiss was meant for them alone. It was so real. She was lost in his touch, his kiss, and the whole room disappeared, as if the entire world stopped around them.

The ringing of her cellphone caused a sudden interruption. Gwen fought the urge to answer but realizing the mood was already broken, she gave in. Maxine. Who else would it be?

"I'm so sorry, David. Excuse me for just one minute."

David watched Gwen sprint away from the dance floor. He stood in a frozen stance, his hands in his pockets, clearly amazed at what just happened.

"What is it, Maxine?" Gwen demanded, struggling to withhold her annoyance.

"Gwen, I know you're having doubts about going to the party, but I really need to talk to you." The tone of her voice was more grave and strangely less cheerful.

"Is there something wrong?" Gwen said in concern.

"Well, Chace is looking a lot rough than usual. What happened between you two?"

"Oh god, I can't even speak about it."

"Don't worry. It's best if we talk in person."

Gwen helplessly looked at David. "I've got other plans."

"Honey, I promise you, it won't take long" Maxine persisted. "I just...don't want you to get hurt..."

Gwen's eyes narrowed in confusion. "Maxine, what's going on?"

"Meet me at the Waldorf Astoria. I'll be there."

Gwen clicked off the phone. She was deeply reluctant. She didn't want to leave this place. She didn't want to leave David. She could feel the flutter in her heart and knew he felt the same. But there was this thing called unfinished business. And if Chace was there, well, she had to step up to him, even though she never wanted to see his face again.

Gwen returned to the bar to find Vera uncharacteristically flirting with the shaved head, tattooed bartender.

"Am I interrupting something?" Gwen chuckled.

"Oh no." Vera beamed. "This is Clark."

The tall, handsome bartender cocked a polite nod and made a sexy grin. Even Gwen couldn't help but blush.

"Leaving so soon?"

"Maxine wants to have a little girls' time. So just drop by at the house when you're, uh, finished here. Trust me, I won't be long."

Vera focused her attention back to Clark. "You can have all the time in the world."

Gwen smiled and turned to look for David. She faced him, not wanting to leave without saying two words to him. Or maybe even those three words with the words "like" or possibly "love" in between them.

"You're leaving?" David said, his brown eyes asking her to stay.

"I...I have to leave." Gwen had that same yearning in her heart, too. She wished the night could go on longer. She held his hand, feeling the warmth of his touch. And then let go.

As she walked out the door, she gazed at David one last time.

"I'll be seeing you."

A GIRL'S INTUITION

"In my guest bedroom, Shawnie? How gross."

Maxine and Shawnie were lounging in the lobby of the Waldorf Astoria, discussing Shawnie's recent rendezvous with Blake Kingston. Maxine could not bear to hear any more.

"It wasn't what you think." Shawnie giggled. "It was special. It was romantic."

"Call it what you want," Maxine retorted. "Having your little interlude in my nicely primed guest room, at a party no less, is not a sign of class in my book. And that Blake Kingston seems like a total sleazeball."

Shawnie flipped her hair haughtily. "Well, you have your opinions about him and I'll have mine."

Not soon after, the girls eyed Rain Bosworth, the ultimate queen bee, ruler of the senior class, with her customary clique. Maxine had heard of Rain from word of mouth and only seen her from afar. But here was the big showcase. And Maxine sure had a lot to see. At first, she only saw her face in the crowd, her dark brown bangs were long, almost covering her eyes. When Rain shifted the bangs to the side, she wore heavy eye shadow that matched her black lipstick. Breaking out of the crowd, she was dressed in an all- black lace dress, with her short sleeves scrunched up in even more black lace, her hair hemmed up into a cutesy ponytail. Maxine just couldn't help but notice the dress was a tad bit over the top. It was like she stepped out of some twisted fairy tale on acid. Was it supposed to be an avant-garde, Lady Gaga–inspired ensemble? And if Maxine noticed, she was certain a lot of other people had, too.

There was no doubt the girl was losing her golden touch. And since this was the last of her ruling years, there was no turning back. But in the meantime, Maxine would be happy to take her place.

Maxine dug through her small purse and glanced at her cellphone, checking the time. "I have some business to attend to. If you want to look for lover boy, go as you please," she told Shawnie.

Maxine scanned the room to see if there was anyone important. Boom. Chace Fairbanks materialized in her distant gaze, a bit scruffy in his Badgley Mischka tuxedo. Just her luck.

Two hands wrapped around Maxine's hips before she could catch her breath. Lips brushed up against her ear.

"Guess who?"

Maxine recognized the voice instantly. She didn't know if tonight was the right time to break it off with Austin, but there was no beating around the bush. She was known to be a heartbreaker back in Statesville, so she didn't see why this would be a problem. You meet with a guy one day and then you work your way over to the next another day. That was how she rolled; she kept her options open. There was another reason to end things, something Maxine didn't like to contemplate too deeply: Austin reminded her of herself a little too much. Particularly, some qualities she didn't like, but in her opinion, it was too hard to change. Seeing these qualities in the guy she liked wasn't giving her a peace of mind.

As if on cue, Maxine shook off her thoughts, put on a cavalier face, and turned to Austin. But once she saw the twinkle in his green eyes, she softened. "Austin, sweetie, this isn't working out. I know we've been dating, for like, a week or so, but I don't see how this can go any further. It's not you, it's me. I know that sounds trite but it's true. I really need to be *mature* to go steady with someone, and I'm just not. Again, I'm sorry."

Maxine rushed away before Austin could say a word. If there was any guilt plaguing her system, she would brush it off with a flick of a wrist. She was a newly minted New Yorker, a girl of insolence, and in her judgment, hearts were meant to be broken.

Maxine was making her way to the entrance, but not without a glance of what she was seeing.

Chace was practically all over Bianca, kissing her neck, fondling her breasts, and groping every part of her body. *What a double-crossing asshole.* To think that she was one of the few girls who actually *thought* he was perfect. She had to tell Gwen...No, she had to show Gwen what a brazen animal he'd become. The way he mounted at her like a dog chasing a bone, was revolting. Everybody had their full attention on them and he didn't care, leading Bianca up the stairs to a hotel room. It was such a sloppy display of arrogance. Maxine knew she made a mistake. She quickly dialed Gwen's number.

Gwen arrived fifteen minutes later outside the hotel entrance, leaning beside the gargoyle statues. "I'm here. What's the hurry? And please, no surprises. I had enough those."

Maxine took a moment but then caught her breath through the crisp night air. "I saw Chace and..."

From Gwen's reaction, Maxine begin to wonder what Chace had actually done. Was he that much of an asshole beneath the surface?

"Gwen, what happened that night?" Maxine asked, curiously. "You never really told about the date, and from my best friend instinct, something probably went seriously wrong."

"I'll keep this short and simple," Gwen answered briskly. "He got drunk, tried to force himself on me, and I, immensely repulsed by him, went off to collect my thoughts."

"Geez Gwen," Maxine said, taken aback. "I guess this wasn't the first time he fell off the wagon."

"Maxine, what are you getting at?"

Maxine held out her hand. "Come on. I know you're not going to like this but you gotta get those feelings out somehow."

J. D. Fitzgerald

IT'S MY PARTY AND I CAN CRY IF I WANT TO

Bianca observed the ballroom down below the staircase, sipping her glass of wine in satisfaction. So here it was. Now presenting, the Kiss the Stars extravaganza at Waldorf-Astoria. If she wanted to break out of Hamilton, why not go out with a bang?

"Bianca, I've just gotten word that the CEO of 'Save the Dolphins' charity fund is headed your way," sophomore Maggie Tarlston mechanically informed her.

"Is everything running smoothly?"

Maggie bopped her head forward like a secret service agent. "It's all good."

"Okay, just make sure to check over the signature list." *Well, if anybody cares to donate that is,* Bianca thought cynically.

"I'm on the go," Maggie responded briskly as she strutted away.

She'd had to hand it to Maggie Tarlston, she was a real go-to girl. There was no way in hell that Sondra and especially Isabella could ever match her skill set. Sondra had the smarts but was very lazy, carrying off her usual blasé don't-carish attitude. Isabella would be up in the air, too distracted to keep up with the plans. Depending on those girls were frustrating, even in her most dire of circumstances, she was always stuck in limbo. At first, Bianca had looked down her nose at Maggie, with her distasteful, unflattering wardrobe, including her trademark shoulder-pad blazers that looked straight out of the eighties, and her poofy, untamed hair hoisted up in a less than competent ponytail.
However, Bianca eventually came to overlook the physical and focus on the internal. She realized how smart and attentive Maggie was to her duties and, in her intuition, Bianca looked between the lines to the people who were loyal to her.

From primal instinct, she spotted Sondra and Isabella having a grand o'l time with Tara Broskowski. So, these were their new friends now. The obnoxious hillbilly, the dimwitted Valley girl, and the Jersey Shore reject. If things could get any worse. Bianca was incensed. Who the hell invited her? That Triffendorf girl had the nerve to drag over her skanky friends to the party. Typical. How could one person, a nobody from Backwoods, USA, mind you, take away the two people that she, at least, thought she knew all her life and throw it up in her face. How the hell did she get so crafty, fomenting an uprising in her social status on her first fucking day of school? How perfect. How fucking perfect. But Bianca kept her cool. She didn't want to cause a scene or bite someone's head off. She needed to handle it the adult way. After all, this *was* a civilized party.

Bianca stepped up to the three girls with ladylike poise. "May I speak to my friends, please?" she said to Tara politely.

Tara gave a curt nod and walked off with a swish of her hair.

Bianca had her focus on Sondra and Isabella, looking them straight in the eye. Annoyance soon turned into disappointment. Ignorance was surely bliss.

"Girls, we need to talk...I'm afraid this is going to be my final party. I'm in the process of transferring from Hamilton."

"So sorry to hear that, Bianca" Sondra replied in her usual sugary fake tone. "What made you come to that decision?"

"Okay, enough with the charade, Sondra," Bianca said unconvinced. "I know you're not gonna miss me all that much, so why won't we just say our goodbyes now."

"Leaving us so soon?" Sondra asked inquisitively.

"I wouldn't worry about my sudden departure, I mean, don't you have Maxine to latch onto?"

"Well, I would say she is much *fun* to be around," Sondra emphasized. "Good luck with your transfer, though."

"We'll send you a postcard," Isabella tittered after.

Then off they went, walking into the crowd like she was an inconvenience to them, as if all their years of friendship was just a speck in the wind, leaving Bianca in bleak oblivion. She was so despondent and dazed. She'd lost her friends to a phony they'd just met a few weeks ago. There was nothing. Nothing to look back from. She had no friends. No boyfriend. No appreciation from her parents or schoolmates. All she wanted to do was crawl up in a corner somewhere. She had thoughts of contemplating about drowning her sorrows. At first, she was only an occasional drinker, but it was like Chace's habits were the only thing left of his memory.

As Bianca made her way to the bar, she was intercepted by a middle-aged woman in a bright red suit with her brownish blond bob cut from cheek to cheek. Once she locked eyes with Bianca, she beamed with a perky smile.

"Are you Bianca Walworth?" the woman asked in a merry tone.

Bianca stared at the woman like an idiot. "Yes." She continued to the bar when suddenly the woman announced, "I'm Julie Sullivan, founder of the 'Save the Dolphins' fund."

Bianca stopped her tracks. Right. Maggie had told her a while ago that the CEO was arriving. Crap. She had to put her personal problems aside and get in the grove of her business priorities.

She put on a serious face and checked herself in order.

"Please take a tour. Have some hors d'oeuvres," Bianca presented to the woman.

"Oh no, sweetheart. All I want is to congratulate you on this very fine charity event."

"Thank you, ma'am, it was a pleasure. If you'll excuse me, though, I'm sort of busy." Her voice sounded faint, her expression vacant. Bianca's tone was automatic, but she couldn't quite manage the fake smile needed to hide her crushing grief.

Bianca grabbed a bottle of champagne, perfectly chilled to her delight. She sat in the nearest corner where nobody could see her, deep in the shadows. She took a long swig, tasting the sizzling, cooling liquid. She wanted to forget. Forget how empty she felt. Was there any shoulder left to cry on? Her thoughts were lapsing in with the alcohol. God, she was turning into a wreck.

Bianca wandered around the party, as if a part of her soul was being drifted into elsewhere. Her mind was becoming more and more transparent, swallowed down in a blurry daze.

"You ought to be ashamed!" said a woman's sharp voice.

Bianca turned around, slightly confused. "Wha—what?"

It was Julie Sullivan, a few minutes later. The rose in her cheeks disappeared into a pale, angry expression. Her arms were folded firmly across her chest, in authoritative fashion. She looked Bianca square in the eye. Her optimistic reliance was now gone, and Bianca was a bit too tipsy to understand why she was so upset.

"I never thought a girl like you, with a such a prominent, upstanding background, would throw a wild teenage party."

Bianca rubbed her temples. "What are you talking about?" she said, her voice hoarse and a little slurred.

"I found gin, vodka, and beer bottles in the garbage can," the woman ranted. "I also saw two of your party guests in a very inappropriate position."

Just when Bianca was going to ask who the party guests were, she glanced over to the other side of the room and saw Blake Kingston run out of the girls' bathroom, tagging along a girl who didn't look anything like the blonde he'd been keeping company with.

Son of a bitch, Bianca scolded in her head. Of course, he would be the one who could truly ruin her party. Why the hell had she invited him? What purpose does she serve to *these* people? But she realized, there was no morals to be had. No self-control. No cares in the world at all because they were invincible, shielded in front of powerful legacies to keep their reputations intact. It was insulting.

"Hello, young lady, I'm talking to you!" the woman leaned over and sniffed Bianca. "Oh god, I can smell the booze on you, too. Just wait until your father hears about this. And don't think I don't know who he is because I do!"

Bianca's emotions were building up so rapidly. The anguish, the agony, the humiliation, it was all too much for her. She didn't hold back. There was no need to.

"Fuck off!"

"How dare you!" Julie Sullivan said in horror. "Just you remember I'll keep my word about this," she added threateningly.

"Did I not speak loud enough? Get the hell out!"

The woman stiffly turned her head, marching to the door.

Bianca blinked, twirling around; her black evening dress glittered in shame.

Everybody watched. They were the perfect audience, enjoying a delightful display of self-destruction right before their eyes. The once golden girl of Hamilton Academy, bright, beautiful, would-be success, had lost her Midas touch. Tears welled in Bianca's eyes; she shielded her face, so nobody would see the broken-down look she wore. This was where she would end it all. End this party. End this incredibly awful night. But no. She wanted to run. Forget it all. Let everyone else worry about their own troubles.

She started to run up the stairs but bumped into Chace, who smelled of his favorite lime liquor.

"Hey, babe," he crooned, his alcohol-fueled breath stinging Bianca's eyes.

"Chace get out of my way," Bianca said in a low, icy tone of irritation.

She turned and came back down the stairs and into the lobby, her arms crossed, protecting herself, but Chace grabbed her around the stomach, stopping her tracks.

Bianca looked away, not letting him see her tear-stained face. "What do you want from me?" she sighed in defeat.

"Come on, you're my one and only. Can't I hold you?" Chace whispered sensually in her ear.

Bianca's body weakened, getting lost in his touch. *Mmm,* how she missed his touch. Her emotions were taking over now. There was no going back. The memories of what they had was strong. She didn't want to go back to him, she didn't want to be hurt again, but it was hard to resist his unquenchable lust. She yearned for this for so long that the heartbreak, the anger, and the resentment she had against him, all but vanished.

He held onto Bianca, her face buried in his chest as they carried up the stairs of her booked hotel room. He laid Bianca gently on the bed, caressing every pleasurable part of her soul. Her body sizzled in response, enveloping his lips to hers.

But there were two knocks on the door. *Fuck, who could this be?*

Maxine trailed up the stairs, leading Gwen to the hotel room, hearing sounds coming from the third room. She placed her ear to the door. Ugh, she could hear all that panting from way over here. Maxine knocked on the door two times.

"Room service!"

Bianca whipped the door open. Maxine scanned her up and down. Though she was still well put-together, Bianca was a bit worn out. Smeared mascara was brushed over her cheeks, her hair a bit rumpled.

"Geez, girl, what happened to you?" Maxine said with smug repugnance.

Bianca seethed in anger. "What the hell are you doing here?"

Chace sat up from the bed. He slowly turned his head, peeking through the cracked door. "Gwen?"

Gwen emerged from the shadows with a stoic expression. She just knew she was going to step into a scene like this. She was warned about this guy twice, but there was no use. She had to learn it the hard way. To see what it was like to be on other side of team and gaining nothing in the process.

As Chace slowly walked up to her, all Gwen could see was her father's face. His steel blue eyes under-laced with red veins. The tears. The screaming. The abandonment. It was all building up in her again. What did she see in this guy? A guy who reminded her so much of her father, bounded in his reckless consumption? He wasn't the slick, suave, smooth Prince Charming that she'd thought he was. He was nothing more than a messy, sloppy, pathetic drunk. She had enough of this bullshit.

Gwen peered at Chace in fierce concentration and, in sheer force, she pushed him down to the ground. She ran out the room and into the curious crowd of party guests. Maxine followed right after.

Chace remained on the floor, staring at the ceiling. He sat up in a fetal position, his eyes pleading to Bianca. "I...I don't know what's going on?"

He'd had his first drink when he was thirteen, never stopping since. And Bianca, the ever-dutiful girlfriend, had watched time and again as Chace made a complete ass of himself, with no memory of what had happened the next day. Each time she would briskly put her feelings aside and still see Chace as the future Ivy League boyfriend she'd come to love. However, now that they were separated, Bianca had the opportunity to see his true colors. It was definitely ugly.

She left the hotel key on the coffee table and stood by the door. "Chace...get some rest."

Bianca slowly and carefully walked down the stairs, ignoring her party guests. Just as she predicted, everyone went into a frenzy, squabbling, gawking, and pulling out their cellphones. *Oh yes, yes, yes, eat it up, you fucking vultures!*

She stormed out of the hotel and continued down the sidewalk, grabbing the first taxi she could find. Once she climbed inside, she leaned her head back, hoping she could scream out her frustration but she had to keep the little control that she had, although she was slowly losing her grip. Suddenly, a wave of calm swept over her. She breathed slowly and closed her eyes. The show was finally over. What now? What would become of her? She couldn't bear to show her face at school. All she wanted to do was disappear, waiting for the day to arrive at her new boarding school unscathed. Facing problems was not the way to go, but that was the hardship of being a teenager. Ever since freshman year, Bianca had tried to carry herself in a mature way. But the walls had broken down, and she felt as lonely and insecure as ever.

By the time she got home, it was quiet, still, and motionless. Dad spending time with colleagues. Mom at one of her fashion banquets. Bianca collapsed in her bed, sobbing uncontrollably. Everything was falling down at her feet, not sure how she could pick up the pieces. Thoughts were running in Bianca's head but slowly, calmly, she drifted off to sleep, letting all the negative energy wash away.

J. D. Fitzgerald

THE CASUALTIES OF LOVE

It happened. She hadn't even wanted to go to that stupid party, but she accepted her fate. And in some strange twisted way, it had to happen. Gwen needed clarity that Chace wasn't right for her. He was a rich kid with no limits. As cliché as that sounded, that's just the way things were. His lifestyle was too fast paced, along with his capacity to down every liquor bottle he could find. But it was over. It was finally over. It was time for some re-evaluating; Gwen was ready to relinquish her girlish daydreams. Life could be ordinary, but life could be not. Life could be extraordinary, but life could be not. Having hopes and disappointments is a hard thing to balance, but Gwen always knew how to escape her emotions with writing. Just write out whatever what was eating her inside and turn it into something positive. She wasn't sure if she could reveal herself yet but having those thoughts to herself could be worth the wait.

She came into the living room and saw Susan, Mona, and Vera already settled into the couch, side by side, watching Netflix and eating popcorn. How adorable. Gwen squeezed in between them, giving out a hearty giggle. She decided to wipe the slate clean. She had her mom. She had her friends. There was not anything more in the world to accommodate her emotional stability; It was all through self-healing and reassurance. That's what Gwen needed. That's what Gwen wanted.

Later in the bedroom, Gwen sat by the window, channeling the lyrics of Red Hot Chili Peppers' "Scar Tissue," playing on her radio. Such an appropriate song for the evening.

"So, Mona, how did it go with Matilda?" Vera asked, lounging on the plush beanbag.

Mona, deep in thought, had a lopsided smirk; there was a look of regret yet relief. "I...just couldn't do it."

Suddenly the revelation caught Gwen's attention. "Mona, you dreamed about this all your life. What changed your mind?"

"I didn't really change my mind," Mona responded. "I still have time on my hands, things to experience and learn from. I just can't leap forward and then leap right back. I'm still young. Any moment can happen in a lifetime."

Mona's words were filled with such wisdom. From the sensational magic she brought on stage, she had a chance, grasping it at the palm of her hand. Touring with a rock band, selling shows, crashing hotel rooms, revealing herself through her art, her music. But she gave all that up, just to have a sense of normality in her life.

Gwen walked over and hugged Mona hard. "You know I'm always there for you."

She rested her head on Gwen's shoulder. "Always and forever."

Vera jumped in, almost knocking the girls over; the three of them could barely contain their laughter. "Well, don't leave me hangin'," Vera joked while tickling Mona's underarms.

A few minutes later, Kyle entered the room, looking simple but still sophisticated in a blue turtleneck and denim jeans. Her green emerald eyes darted straight at Gwen. *Uh-oh, here comes a lecture.* Although she had her usual stern expression, there was a deep concern. She sat with Gwen, a playful arch to her eyebrow.

"I saw what happened, but you could've heard warning bells from a mile away," Kylie assured her. "I'm telling you, it's not surprising that a guy who gets that much attention would be a little unstable."

Gwen waved her off. "I know I fucked up, there's no to need tell me."

"I hate to say this but—"

"I told you so," both girls said in unison.

Suddenly, Vera jolted up from the bed as if a spark been plugged into her. "Oh shit!"

"What's wrong, Vera?" Gwen asked, as the girls looked on in slight confusion.

Vera reached in her pocket and gave Gwen a folded-up piece of paper. "I meant to give you this earlier. It's a poem from David."

Gwen opened the letter... and she savored every word.

His writing was so undeniably passionate. She never thought a boy could harbor such strong feelings towards her. The way he described about her was ethereal and heartfelt, she wondered why she didn't reciprocate any sooner.

How could she have been so stupid? There was someone waiting for her this whole time, yet she'd been caught in this web of desire, desire to fit in, desire to be liked, desire to be someone she wasn't and would never be. Maxine had pushed her further into the temptations of the Upper East Side, but it was her own her gullibility that left her stuck in a loop. If only she could find a way to make it up to David, express her feelings as beautifully as he did.

"I need to see him," Gwen blurted out.

"At school maybe," Vera suggested.

"No," Gwen said, thinking to herself. "It has to be somewhere special."

"Empire State Building?" Kylie queried

"Coney Island?" Mona added. "It has a good view of the city."

For a lingering moment, Gwen's mind blinked. "How about somewhere in Brooklyn? Mansfield Park?"

Vera nodded her head in agreement. "Great choice. David always hangs out there after nine."

Gwen gazed out her window again, dreaming of what was to be. She was thinking of what to say to him, how to say it. His words were so rich with admiration, how would she ever describe anything special about him? But there was something special. His generosity, his kindness, the way his lips curled when he smiled, and especially those beautiful brown eyes that would light up gold.

This was her chance to finally tell him how she felt.

"I like him," Gwen said. "I really, really like him."

Vera laid her hand on top of Gwen's. "Then tell him."

"I will...I will."

Shawnie stood in front of the door to Blake's apartment suite. She took a big inhalation and let out a huge exhalation. She'd heard those awful rumors Maxine and the girls told her. Was it true? Was she just some plaything Blake could use when he wanted to? She had to get to the bottom of it, get answers out of him, although her fragile state of mind prevented her from being confrontational.

She hesitated in the hallway, her hand trembled once she touched the steel doorknob. Shawnie heard chatter and occasional feminine laughter, making her stomach turn over. She felt like she was crashing a party, and, as she was usually the life of the party, it was kind of ironic, but still a weird situation.

Two knocks on the door and Blake popped out with his sly grin and his wrinkled button-down, sleeves up to his elbows, and leaning casually on the doorway.

"Well, hello, miss," Blake said in a low, sexy croon, smoothing back his not-so-slick black hair, which was messy all over. Shawnie could tell by his bloodshot eyes he'd been partying a little too hard, not to mention this was the night of the Kiss the Stars party…at two in the morning.

Still. Still, she wanted to mesh into him once again, yet she stopped her thoughts from progressing any further.

Shawnie peeked inside the room to see who the party guests were. She glimpsed at the same girl Blake had been fooling around with. She matched Isabella's description perfectly: Long straight black hair, European features, legs like a gazelle, and a short, tight dress up to her derriere. Shawnie hid in the hallway, feeling too small and insecure to stand next to a girl like that.

"You want to join us, babe?" Blake offered.

"I'd rather talk to you alone," Shawnie said, keeping her composure.

"No prob." Blake moved into the hallway and shut the door behind him. He immediately sauntered toward her and rubbed his fingertips against her shoulders lightly.

"Ready to get down the business?" Blake whispered in her ear, nuzzling her neck.

Shawnie squirmed away, turning to face him. "Actually, I have to ask you about something."

Blake folded his arms but kept grinning. "What's there to ask?"

"I've been hearing some rumors that…that you did some sexual things to a girl in the bathroom of the Waldorf hotel tonight." Shawine knew she sounded like a first grader but at least she'd managed to say it.

Blake stared at her, perplexed. "Now how did this come out?" he wondered with a chuckle.

"Don't beat around the bush, Blake," Shawnie retorted, finally getting some strength in her voice.

Blake kept turning away, stifling chuckles as if he couldn't believe he was being interrogated. "Do you actually believe anything those girls say?"

"I don't have to believe a word. I saw you with her. Do you really think I'm that stupid?"

Blake stood there, speechless. He answered her question just by the look on his face. There was no way he was going to smooth talk his way out of this one.

"You do, don't you?" Shawnie said in a soft, embattled tone.

"What did you expect?" Blake said defensively.

"I expected more from you." Shawnie turned away from him. She thought she'd felt something special. A feeling of love at first sight. But that feeling was gone. The sensation of love had been nothing more than lust in the dust.

Blake kept a straight face, although he softened a bit. "We got together one night. Why do I feel like I'm in the hot seat suddenly?"

Shawnie turned back around, her innocent blue eyes turning into an icy, incisive stare. "Because I thought it was special...But I guess it wasn't. You can go back to your party now."

Shawnie walked off, holding back tears of heartbreak. This was what she got. This was exactly the result of reading those cheesy romance novels and fairy tales, trapped beyond her blissful days of the California west coast. It was silly of her to find love in the big apple, but she was deep into her heart than above her head. Even if she'd once thought Blake was the epitome of the aristocratic gentleman, the lack of judgment she set against him, soon surfaced. Blake Kingston wasn't her Prince Charming. He was a self-indulgent sleazeball. Though for now, Shawnie needed Maxine more than she ever would. On the other hand, boys were definitely off her radar.

J. D. Fitzgerald

* *

JUST ANOTHER DAY AT SCHOOL

The following day at school was endlessly hectic as the gossip surrounding the Kiss the Stars party intensified. Word after word, text after text, it was inescapable.

Gwen found enough courage to face what was coming. She no longer groveled in embarrassment when put on the spot and always reminded herself of this special little saying, *if worst comes to worst, if your nerves start to burst, let it be known, your pride will come first.* It was a rhyme her mom would say to her on her first day of kindergarten. Today that little ditty was to be put in good use. Gwen had a new sense of confidence...and a new sense of style. A cropped black sleeveless jacket over a Sex Pistols T-shirt, tight blue jeans, and her favorite pair of skater shoes with her blond hair flowing freely down her shoulders. This day, she finally emerged as the woman she wanted to be—and she'd never felt better.

"Oh my god, it was such an epic failure," Gwen heard a girl whispered. "I wasn't surprised she ended the night with pity sex."

"Too bad for her," the other girl responded. "Chace just can't seem to make up his mind. I heard his rebound girl had an eyeful when she entered their hotel room. I swear, it's like something out of a shitty teen drama."

Gwen had a smirk on her face. Let them all gossip, it would die down eventually. Gwen proudly put on her dark shades and flaunted her walk of victory. Whether the popular vote of her peers supported her or condemned her, she was fully aware of her self-worth.

In the cafeteria, Gwen joined the girls at the table, noticing Shawnie sitting in the center, her bright smile gleaming splendidly.

"You seem quite happy today," Gwen said.

"Just keeping my spirits up," Shawnie replied, her smile turning into a strained grin.

"How come?"

"Blake wasn't...exactly the guy I expected him to be."

Gwen reassured her. "Don't worry. Sometimes it takes a while for a guy to mature into a relationship. It's complicated, I know."

"I guess I'm a fool for love."

"Just focus on you and all will be in your favor," Gwen encouraged. "Be sure of that."

Gwen looked over and stared at the empty table where Bianca gained her supremacy. Now that her pride was shattered in defeat, she chose not to face the outcome of her humiliation. Gwen was relieved that Chace was nowhere to be found. If she saw either presence grace the halls of school, it would only sour her solitude.

But through the following weeks being wrapped in the sordid lives of her privileged classmates, Gwen stood above the surface of caged indifference. *So what. Better them than me.* Gwen was quite comfortable of being just a regular kid. Yes, a kid. Not quite a woman but getting there eventually.

Maxine strutted down the hallway with her three companions, Sondra, Tara, and Isabella, joining at her side. Her mission finally completed. There was still a long way to go but at least she'd made her mark.

Maxine burst into the cafeteria, making sure everybody took note of her customary white suit tailored suit with a silver sequin top. Oh yes, she was the star of the show and everybody had to take cover. The first row of the second table was her territory, succession reaching at her fingertips. Maxine had enough room to get one more girl to rule at her side. She spotted Shawnie, sitting at Gwen's table.

"I'll catch up with you, girls," Maxine said, walking to the table.

Maxine, surprising even herself, sat down at Gwen's table.

Awkward silence loomed. Mona gave Maxine the evil eye. Kylie, a quiet nod. Vera, a confused arch of the eyebrow.

"Okay, I know you don't want me to sit here. Just coming to say hi," Maxine explained, getting up from the table.

Gwen grabbed her hand. "Maxine, wait. We're not trying to throw you under a bus or anything. If you want to go form your own clique, it's fine. Just be happy where you are, okay."

Maxine smiled. Then she looked at Shawnie with urgency in her eyes. "Shawnie...do you want to join me?"

"Well, of course I wanna join you," Shawnie said with childlike shrillness, jumping up from her seat.

Maxine and Shawnie each blew kisses to the girls, then walked over to their newfound table where Maxine, with great formality, sat right in Bianca's spot.

The girls were discussing plans for next week, just as soon as they noticed a well-dressed boy heading their way. He gazed at Kyle, his wire-rimmed glasses focused steadily in her direction. She thought it was weird how she was getting all this attention from boys all of a sudden, but then again, she'd dated Jeremy Fletcher, one of Hamilton's senior finest, so maybe that had changed a few things.

This guy was amazingly distinguished for a boy in his teens. His dark brown hair was side-parted; his green silk tie was tucked under a dark blue cashmere sweater with khaki pants and well-polished shoes.

His light blue eyes bore into Kyle's emerald green. "Hi, I'd like to introduce myself. I'm Jared Milton, I just transferred from Loomis Chaffee. I'm only here for the tour," the boy said with a winsome British accent.

Kyle made a very perky, giggling laugh, melting off her usual air of stiff, stern aloofness.

"You're Kyle Durmsdale, right?" Jared asked, showing off his alluring smile.

Kyle marveled. "Yes...yes, I am."

"Oh that's fantastic! Bianca told me all about you."

Kyle blinked her eyes in confusion. "Bianca? As in Bianca Walworth?"

"Why, yes. We're actually switching schools at the moment. She says you're a very well-informed girl."

"Did she?" Kyle chuckled skeptically. "Why would she have you speaking to me?"

"Bianca recently stepped down as honor society president; she asked me to take over the work. And the first thing she suggested was to have you as head secretary of the board."

Kyle's face glowed. The words came out so freely. *Head secretary.* She looked at her friends for support. Their exuberant smiles showed how immensely proud they were. Kyle gazed upon Jared, his eyes twinkling gently.

"I thought I was too smart for my own good," Kyle mused.

"Bianca seems to have faith in you. She said you have what it takes to get the job done," Jared reassured her. "Maybe we can sit with the other members to discuss this further?"

The girls threw sly looks at Kyle, making her blush as she walked off with Jared.

"It's just so odd how guys magically come to us these days," Vera joked. "Have our boobs grown bigger all of a sudden?"

"That is what I call the main feminine source," Mona said. "Now if only we could use that kind of magic to attract the *right* kind of guy, that would pretty much seal the deal."

The right kind of guy. Gwen was well prepared for tonight's plan...but first she had to clean up the mess between her and Chace. This time with no audience.

J. D. Fitzgerald

◆ * *

FADED GLORY

With each item of clothing folded in a neat pattern, Bianca placed them in her brown leather suitcase. She sat down on the bed, looking at the floor. She had to do this. No questions asked. She had to recuperate, to start over and gain what was lost.

She had spent half of last week, vehemently searching the web, hoping to find a boarding school to transfer to. It was the only way to salvage her dignity, after being irretrievably ostracized at Hamilton. She wanted someplace private. Very, very private. Someplace distant. Someplace where nobody could have any physical insight of her.

Loomis Chaffe Boarding School was the right choice, however, on one condition...the location on the search engine was a student exchange website. It was sort of a Facebook for private school students. Bianca searched hard to find the perfect student to switch with. The person had to have pride, resilience, and the balls to deal with those callous brats.

She found her perfect match in Jared Milton. By the look of his picture, she knew he was a sufficient candidate. His strong-willed face showed he had a mighty invisible armor, like nothing would stand in his way. His credentials were not far from amazing, excelling in extracurricular activities, including...honor society. Also, a bonus point for being a senior, which would give him the opportunity to nominate himself as president.

His online status was bright green, juicing up her excitement. Bianca instantly clicked two times. They kept in contact by the end of the week, discussing their schools, the pros, cons, comparisons, and contrasts. Bianca was certain there was to be an equal compromise to the proceedings.

Once Jared emailed her the photos of the school landscape, Bianca was exhilarated. The gray stone construction was built like an ancient castle, newly remodeled, newly substantial. Much more prestigious than Hamilton. Inside was even more gorgeous, with comfortable bedrooms, wide historical study rooms, a fancy dining room with a lascivious sixteenth-century French setting and the amazing window view of the pine tree forest. It was pure heaven.

She was scheduled to meet Jared at the Penn station on Saturday afternoon. He was much more handsome than his photo, wearing a blue sports jacket under a black button-down and black khakis. Though for some reason, he didn't seem to be her type, reminding her of Stanley Woodbruck, her studious but inept junior counsel at Honor society, who was too much into his schoolwork to have time for girlfriends. However, this was a business proposition, not a date. Although, Jared did sneak a flirty glance at her.

The two of them made plans over coffee at Starbucks. During their conversation, something came to Bianca. She surveyed Jared's intelligent eyes and blue blood physiognomy. He was wise beyond his years, having developed an articulate, sharp British wit. Soon, she realized this guy could be a good match for Kyle. But she not only wanted to play the role of matchmaker, she also wanted to give Kyle the chance to really put herself out there by initiating her to the highest realms of honor society. Bianca saw that she had potential, enough much potential to carry a whole classroom. Who knew what she might think of Bianca now. It was her own jealously that had got the best of her. But this was Bianca's way of finding forgiveness. Not only for others, but for herself.

So it was all set. Bianca's bags were packed, her books were stacked, and the door was open.

Her parents were sitting in the living room. There was the usual coldness in the air, a feeling so hard for her to bear any longer. Just looking at the image of her parents, carelessly lounging in the living room of the ancient townhouse produced an unwelcoming aura. Marla was in the dark gray sitting chair, her jewelry gleaming in the shadows. Nick was standing beside her, his stoned expression gazing a mile away.

"I wish you would've told us this sooner, young lady," Nick said sternly.

"I thought it would be best if I saved you the embarrassment of what I did," Bianca said regretfully.

"You don't have to do this, Bianca," Marla said in her usual blasé tone. "We talked things out with the charity coordinator. We made sure this was all a huge misunderstanding."

Bianca sat down on the sofa. "I'm not changing my mind, Mom. What's done is done."

Strange how they would come to her defense, fix everything they could. But the decision was made. She was not going back to Hamilton to be some laughingstock.

And here was the problem, too. This house was so depressing. The numb of neglect weighed heavy on her.

Two honks sounded outside. Bianca stood up with a suitcase in each hand.

"The cab's here. I have to go," Bianca said softly.

Marla gave Bianca a firm hug, though not too touchy-feely. Nick clasped her shoulder with a strong grip, since it wasn't in his nature to be affectionate.

Bianca Walworth walked out of the house and into a new world. Whatever path was near her way, she prayed, within her hearts of hearts, to find the happiness that she so desperately yearned for.

CENTRAL PARK BLUES

Gwen stared at the pond, the watery waves of her reflection glittering under the moonlight. She was thinking of what to say and how to say it. The cool summer air made her even more nervous.

She took another glance at the pond; this time she saw a shadow walking forward. Gwen turned around. Chace was as clean and polished as ever, with his hair slicked back, wearing his blue sweater vest over a white button-down with neatly pressed slacks, looking like the gentleman he'd once seemed. But looks can be deceiving—no matter how primed and debonair someone appeared, an alcoholic is an alcoholic.

Gwen walked up to him, searching for words to function in her brain. A simple "Hi" was what came out.

Chace sheepishly had his hands in his pockets. "Hi."

She looked into his eyes. They were clear, radiating that familiar midnight blue. She turned away cautiously. She didn't want to fall into them again, not after all that had happened. She had never broken up with boy before, much less one who was so charismatic and alluring. But there was always something in the way of being *too* perfect. And from what Gwen witnessed, it was a heavy burden on her.

"Chace...we really need to talk," Gwen said with a sad smile to ease the tension.

"If there's anything you want to hear, I'll explain," he said with worried eyes.

 Gwen gazed down to the ground, taking a moment. "This can't go on any longer."

Chace nodded his head dolefully. "I understand. I wish I could control myself, but it's too late."

Gwen put a reassuring hand on Chace's face. The expression he held affected her. She didn't know what he was feeling inside or why he drank the way he did. She hadn't had the chance to really and truly get to *know* him.

"Chace, you need to get help," Gwen consoled.

"I know I do. Sometimes when I drink, it conflicts with my emotions. It's like I'm in this tiny little ball of combustion."

The memories of Gwen's father stung her once more. "I know," Gwen realized. "There's something I didn't tell you before...my father is an alcoholic."

"I'm sorry to hear that," Chace said, looking incredibly miserable.

Gwen took his hands into hers, immersed in his empathy. "Don't feel bad. It's just...I couldn't witness that again. For my sake and yours, I think it's for the best."

There were positives to their short-lived relationship. Like how they'd spent time on this very same spot, talking about their childhoods, their dreams, and what they wanted out of life. However, that was the only good memory Gwen could ever think of.

"I guess this is it." Chace strayed his head at the trees. The air of the evening was so devastating.

For one last moment, Gwen had a chance for salvation. "Just one more thing. There's someone I want you to meet at Carlye's. I think it might be a benefit for you."

"Gwen...good luck."

"Thanks."

Gwen waved goodbye, lifting the weight off her shoulders. She checked her watch. Now her heart lies with where it surpassed. Nothing was standing in her way now. This was her moment. This was her chance. Mansfield Park. Just a subway ride away. And David would be there.

Maxine was becoming terribly impatient, sitting at the bar table at Carlye's. She'd gotten a text from Gwen to meet here at the pool table, but she was nowhere to be found.

Maxine was going to wait five more minutes and then off she goes. *That's a good one, Gwennie.*

When Maxine glanced at the entrance door, Chace Fairbanks, of all people, came in. Once he caught Maxine's glance, it looked like Chace was heading her way. *Holy crap.* She had a chill down her spine. When was the last time a guy did that to her? Ever? She'd been so busy setting him up with Gwen, even though she was the one who had the hots for him. Chace was just so enticing, so magnetic. He was smooth and liquid with his approach, blending in with his impeccable good looks. But there was some heavy lifting to be pulled off from his...habit. Not everybody's perfect but Maxine knew how to handle things.

He sat down beside her. Maxine could feel his body heat from a mile away.

"Hey," Chace said in a low, weary voice.

"Hi."

There was silence between them, hearing the faint sounds of the jazz band playing. The place sort of set the mood. Or whatever mood Maxine was feeling right now, which was uncontrollable lust. More silence built as the minutes went by. Well, if she was the one to break the silence she just had to darn well do it.

Before she could say anything..."What brings you here?" was Chace's conversation starter.

"I was supposed to meet Gwen but she's nowhere in sight," Maxine replied, feeling a bit bummed.

"Strange, Gwen told me somebody would be waiting for me here as well."

"Oh."

Clever, clever girl. Maxine thought she was the master of the matchmaking game, but it seemed like Gwen was one step ahead of her. Bravo. So what now? Here was Chace, this handsome, elegant boy...with a drinking problem. She didn't want to be the type of girl that could change a man, but what Maxine could do was to clear his mind, raise up his spirits a bit, because, once the timing was right, all she had to deliver was her Southern charm and grace. What Chace needed was a little TLC, and Maxine would gladly give it to him. By the way, he looked kind of down in the dumps.

"I guess we're stuck with each other." Chace chuckled.

"We sure are," Maxine said dreamily, her hand propping up her chin. She just couldn't help herself.

They soon locked eyes. The band was playing an instrumental jazz version of Christopher Cross's "Sailing." Oh yes, it was all set.

Maxine laughed to herself. "My mom played this song so many times."

"Yeah, it reminds me of the ocean." Chace looked out the window regretfully.

Maxine touched his forearm. "What's got you down?"

"I'm such a screwup."

"You can't hold your liquor. It happens all the time. You're not the only poor little rich boy who fell off the wagon. I know from experience." The memories of Maxine entertaining Amber Krecther's dumb college boyfriends resurfaced—recounting that awful night one of them threw up on her new expensive dress she'd purchased from Bebe's. It had been ugly.

Chace stared into nothing. He held his head in disappointment. "I guess I'm just like everybody else."

Maxine gently lifted his chin up. "Don't you worry. I'm gonna turn that frown upside down. 'Cause once I'm done with you, you're gonna be a brand-new person."

"You're really good with words," Chace said doubtfully.

"Nope," Maxine disagreed with an optimistic chirp. "Every word I say is true. 'Cause everything's gonna be alright."

◆ ✳ ✳

HE'S THE ONE

Gwen held her breath, the drums of her heart beating excitedly. Taking the bus across the Brooklyn Bridge and Ninth Street, she finally made it to Mansfield Park, which was just a block away. Once she walked over to the grassy meadows, the landscape was empty. As she trailed further to the park, there was so much land and trees. No pond, no flowers, just plain empty green all around, very different from Central Park. She was going around in circles; it was impossible to find David here.

Making her way to the playground down the hill, she sat at the swing set, gazing at the dark sky. It was shortly after nine. He had to be here. Gwen didn't want to lose hope. Here at this park was what it all boiled down to, their feelings finally mutual. Quiet, calm, and just for the two of them.

"Gwen?"

Suddenly, Gwen looked over her shoulder. She slowly got up, feeling goosebumps. She turned around to see David, a warm smile spread across his face.

"What are you doing here?" David asked hopefully, shyly putting his hands in his jacket.

Gwen looked deep into his eyes. "Let's just say a friend of mine led me here."

"I need to thank her one day."

David beckoned. Gwen reached out, feeling the tenderness of his hand. The moment they touched, there was an instant spark, and a breeze softly moved between them. "I read your poem...it's beautiful."

He pulled Gwen close to him, strumming his fingers through her hair. "*You're* beautiful."

As their lips inched about a mile closer, Gwen slipped on the grassy meadow, pulling David with her to roll on the soft green carpet. Laughing hysterically, they held on, arms wrapped to one another, entranced by the each other's gaze. David slowly, passionately brushed his lips against hers. Gwen melted into his kiss, bliss and exuberance overwhelming her.

"What do you want to do now?" David whispered, caressing her face softly.

Gwen found comfort in his embrace, she couldn't imagine anywhere else she rather be. "Let's just...bathe under the moonlight."

After all the craziness she'd endured in this strange city, in these strange times, Gwen's young life was finally beginning.

J. D. Fitzgerald

ACKNOWLEDGMENTS

I give thanks to my wonderful, amazing editors Sarah Hopkins and Valarie Valentine.
Thank you two for supporting my work and giving me great feedback.
To my beautiful, courageous mother Michelle, who did her best to keep me and my sister
grounded.
To my loving Aunt, Sharon, who taught me the ways of life and love and encouraged my
dream.
To my ever-sensational grandmother, who has a warrior's spirit but uses that strength
with love and compassion.
To my friend and confidant Ivy, who has been there for me, even in my darkest moments.
And lastly to my brave, sincere, and high-spirited big sister Calisa, who always looked out
for me and always did her best.

216

ABOUT THE AUTHOR

J.D. Fitzgerald was born and raised in North Carolina. He has been writing short stories, novellas, and screenplays since the age of fifteen. He hosts a blog, https://thesto-riesofjdandivy.blogspot.com/, where he writes movie and tv reviews. His other hobbies include interpretive dancing, researching astrology, and studying film and television history. Manhattan girls is his first novel in a series of books. He is currently working on the second novel which will come out later this year.